SWEET Magic SONG

FOR LOVE OF FAE TRILOGY - BOOK ONE

OLIVIA HARDIN

Printed in the United States of America

Sweet Magic Song
Copyright © 2013 Olivia Hardin
Cover Design by Once Upon a Time Covers
Formatting by Self Publishing Editing Service

ISBN-10: 0989783839
ISBN-13: 978-0-9897838-3-5

Dedication

To my grandmother, Theresa. Because even though I can't carry a note, you said you loved the "audible vibrations" I used to belt out in your backyard. And also because you made my mom, who in my humble opinion is the best mom ever – but then, I think she must get it honest.

Chapter
ONE

Roon gazed into his mug of beer with a forlorn sigh. The bubbles percolated and churned, and he lifted the mug and swished them around in a circle until his eyes crossed in a daze. He still wasn't sure what the hell he was doing here.

Actually, he knew why he'd crossed over. Devvie had looked at him with those eyes of hers and that lower lip puckered. *How was I gonna say no?* She told him she thought they'd need him to help finish off the Org. He hadn't planned to cross over from the faery realm, but he couldn't very well say no to *her*.

"You're here because you're an idiot, Roon," he murmured under his breath in a disgusted voice.

So he knew that, in the end, those eyes and those lips were the reason he'd come here from the faery realm. They were also the reason he was in this bar. That reason was simply Devvie.

The hunk of meat she was so in love with gave him the evil eye the moment he made a wisecrack about her sexy ass. *We're besties. I mean, just because I'm in love with her doesn't mean I can't continue to tease her.* And it wasn't as if the comment were untrue. Kent knew good and well her ass was sexy. He shouldn't have growled at Roon for saying it when he was the one who got to have it.

Honest-to-a-fault Jill had warned him it would happen. "All you have to do is speak about five words and he'll jump all over you. Kent doesn't play where Devan's concerned."

Jill was wrong. He was pretty sure he'd gotten at least ten words spoken before they'd raised their fists. And then there Devvie was again, those gold-brown eyes glistening up at him, that lip puckering out. She'd broken them up before either of them could take a swing and then asked Rooney to give them a minute. That was when Jill told him where to find this bar.

Now, days later, he found himself coming back to this bar night after night. Devan was working at getting the rescues organized, and he still wasn't sure exactly what she wanted him to do yet. He figured if he was just doing nothing, then why not do it while drinking?

There were a lot of magical folks there. Most of them were witches and warlocks, but he was surprised to also see a number of faeries. Obviously they were ones who'd chosen to remain in the human realm during the Time of Choosing. Hundreds and perhaps a thousand years before, the gates between the faery and human worlds were spelled so that no one could cross between them without being stripped of their powers. The division forced an end to the conflict between the two halves ever since.

But now there was Devvie. Her combination of fae-witch powers made her a sort of gatekeeper between the worlds, so Rooney had a feeling things were about to change on both sides.

Rooney dropped his head and released a forlorn sigh when he saw that his mug was empty. The bartender—a guy he was pretty certain was a shifter of some sort—asked if he wanted another. He shook his head and slipped the guy a few bucks. He figured Jill and Doc must be pretty much made of money because she handed him a wad of "beer money" each evening before he left.

Now he slid his butt off the barstool and looked off towards the back of the bar. He could see a line at the restrooms, so he figured he'd better get in it before his bladder reached maximum capacity.

He bumped into a brunette vamp trying to take his seat. She smiled lasciviously with pointed teeth, and he rolled his eyes. He didn't care for bloodsuckers, although the lovely Jill had grown on him. For a time, he'd thought she could take his mind off Devvie, but that idea died on the vine when he realized she was still pining for her then-dead lover, Doc. Of course now Doc was back and so that was that.

He leaned against the wall outside the restroom and closed his eyes. Why the hell couldn't he wish Devvie away? He could still remember that one kiss. How is it that a person can wait years and years for a moment and then when it finally comes... it's completely wrong? The Women, those freaking banshees, had told him it would be wrong, but he had to try. He hated that *they* were always right. He reached up an arm to rub his neck in consternation and felt his elbow come into contact with someone. Even before he could open his eyes, he heard a female voice yell, "Hey!"

When his gaze focused on her, he was momentarily dumbstruck. Now this was a gal who could make him forget about Devvie.

"Va-va-voom," he muttered as he eyed her up and down. Who would have thought a restroom rendezvous could have such potential? He tapped the dude next to him and motioned with his chin.

"Forget it," the warlock muttered, putting a big hand through his long blond mane. "She's a bounty hunter. You try to tap that and she'll hand your ass to you on a plate."

When Roon finally made his way through the filthy

restroom, the bar was bustling all the more. Patrons gathered around the u-shaped bar, and the prospect of edging his way in there to get another drink wasn't exactly exciting. With a grumbly sigh, he put his hands into the pockets of his jeans and shoved his way to the door.

It was dark out, and he stopped to take in the night sky. Things were so stark here without the flash and brilliance of the faery realm. Still, he felt awed by it, amazed that the stars could still twinkle with beauty even without the super HD luminescence of the sky he was used to. It was lovely. It also made him feel terribly alone.

He caught sight of a blonde across the street, but she didn't look like a paranormal. She eyed him with a coy smile, and he was tempted. She wasn't drop-dead hot, but she was cute enough. He scratched at his chin with his pinky finger and watched her a moment. A guy came out of the shop just across from her, putting his arm around her shoulder. She wormed her way out of his reach, but there was a playful glint in her eyes that clearly warned she was involved with the dude.

Roon huffed a frustrated sigh, turned around, and headed back inside to drink away the memories.

A few hours and several hard drinks later, he wove his way down the sidewalk and away from the bar. He heard a weird sound, something like a bell, and glanced left and right a few times. He sped up his pace, and yet the sound continued to follow him. When he felt a vibration in his left back pocket, he finally realized it was the cell phone Jill had given him.

By the time he pulled the phone out of his pants, it had stopped ringing. It had to be either Jill or Devan, because no one else would have the number. He glanced at the apparatus for a few moments with a confused glare.

"I must be drunker than I thought. How the hell do I call her back on this thing?"

He didn't know which "she" he was talking about—the blonde one who was his friend or the brunette one who was the friend he was in love with. Before he could ponder that, the phone started ringing again. There was a green "Answer" button on the bottom of the touch screen, and he tapped it a few times with his thumb until he hit it just right.

"Yeah."

"Roon, where the hell have you been? I've been calling for over an hour," Jill demanded. Her voice was pitched with worry.

"What, did you think I was going to get into trouble all alone or something?" He laughed and shook his head, but the action threw him off balance, and he almost toppled over. His own clumsiness made him giggle all the more.

"Rooney, Devan's gone."

His heart dropped into his gut and he almost dropped the phone. "What the hell happened? Where did she go?" He started running towards the woods, looking for a secluded place to open the golden door.

"Some creatures just showed up and took her. Charlie called 'em aliens or something. I don't know, but we need you to get back here. We've got a plan... Roon? Roon, what are you doing?"

He wasn't sure what he was doing. He wanted to open the golden door so he could get back to the hospital, but a blob of orange goo appeared at his feet. That certainly wasn't the type of magic he was trying to conjure. He flicked his hand again and this time a portal opened. But on the other side, all he saw was ocean instead of the hospital. He peeked his head inside and salt water sprayed his face.

"Shit!" he cursed. "What the hell?"

"Are you okay? Do you need me to come get you?"

Rooney took a deep breath, closing his eyes and seeking some calm before trying again. "Listen, I need to concentrate a minute, okay? If I don't get there in ten minutes, call me back."

He hit the end button and slipped the phone back into his pocket. Licking his lips, he put his hands out in front of him and slapped his palms together with a smack. After a moment, he rubbed them against each other until they felt warm. Then he released a breath hard enough to puff his cheeks out. "Okay, Roon. You can do this. You can do this."

He coached himself a bit longer. Then with intense concentration, he waved his right hand out in front of him. A golden light appeared as a speck, growing and growing until the door grew to full size. He recognized the hospital hallway in front of him. With a deep sigh of relief, he stepped inside.

The door closed up behind him, and he started down the hallway, weaving left and then right and then left again. He paused when he got to the kitchen, bending his neck to look inside, but found the room empty.

"You're here. Good, because we could use you to collect Nicky and Gerry as soon as they retrieve the box."

He recognized Jill's voice, but when he turned, the first face his eyes focused on certainly wasn't Jill. She was a very young woman with intense black eyes and even blacker hair. Her pink lips were pursed together, and she frowned when he stared at her a little too long.

"Oh, for goodness sakes, Roon. Stop gawking at her, because we don't have time for you to try another round of flirt-with-the-newbie."

His cheeks flamed hot, and he tossed Jill a nasty glare. "Why don't you tell me what's going on?"

"C'mon," she ordered before she took the lead, heading down the hallway. "Charlie called them aliens, but some sort of tubular creatures just appeared, said a few words, and then just disappeared with Devan, Kent and Langson. Gerry thinks one of those tubes was her sister, and so she and Nicky went…"

"He's drunk."

Rooney had been concentrating on following Jill without leaning from side to side. If his balance was questionable before, it was certainly blown when he'd heard that musical voice from the gorgeous "newbie." He fell left and placed a hand against the wall to steady himself.

Hands on her hips, Jill turned and faced him. "Oh, Roon. You are drunk, aren't you?"

At about that time, the shuffling steps of Doc and Jill's friend Charlie moved in their direction, and Jill sighed in relief. Taking Roon's arm, she shoved him down the hallway back in the direction they'd just come.

"What's going on here?" Charlie asked.

"Go with him, Charlie, and get him some black coffee. He needs to sober up, or he'll be worthless to us."

Chapter
TWO

The pounding of her heart in Belle's chest was so strong she thought her body was shuddering with each beat. She could hear the rushing of the blood in her ears such that it drowned out all other sounds in the room. Lena, Jeremy, and Nona were huddled in a corner with the rest of the hospital's children. They were close to each other—a part of the group but still attached to their siblings. She tossed them a reassuring grin and inclined her head to them.

Lena tugged Nona tighter to her side and nodded back. She was such a strong girl, even at the tender age of eleven. Pride welled in Belle's heart.

A hand clutched her shoulder, shaking it to get her attention. Belle leapt a good foot into the air, flashing angry black eyes at her attacker. It was the red-haired faery, Rooney. He grinned at her with one side of his mouth and stepped back with both hands raised defensively. "Easy. I'm not one of the baddies."

"Don't touch me," she hissed. "I don't like to be touched."

"I tried calling your name, but you didn't seem to hear. Got wax in your ears?"

Her frown deepened so much that a pain stabbed at the center of her forehead. *Your third eye*, she could hear Betty saying to her when she was a child. *We need to get you balanced again.* She remembered the Bittners' maid dressing her in purples and lavenders and placing oils on her feet to get her chakra into proper order. Belle wasn't sure if she believed in it, but Betty always made her feel better.

"What do you want?" Belle forced herself back into the moment and growled at Roon.

"I'm going to be just beyond that door. You and the old man will stay in here with the kids, and if something goes wrong, I'll open the golden door for you, got it?"

She nodded and glanced at the open door leading into the hallway. Jill was just beyond, talking with Doc, a serious, intense glare on her face. Bile churned in Belle's stomach.

As soon as Roon had gotten Nicky and Gerry back with some special box that the Org wanted, the entire hospital began hopping with plans for the their arrival. There was supposed to be a "safe room" for the children to hide in upon any sign of danger. Belle didn't like it one bit that, instead of putting them in that room, the group had decided to let the faery guard them.

"Do you know how to protect yourself?" Roon pressed, lifting his chin and looking down his nose at her.

He had an impish look about him, like a little boy trying to be big. "Want me to show you how I can defend myself?" Her words were low and laced with menace.

He surprised her by laughing. It was a loud, boisterous sound that bounced off the walls of the tiny room. Charlie, though he couldn't have heard their conversation, glanced over at them and chuckled, too, as if the faery's laughter was contagious.

"I can defend myself, faery."

He winked and made a clicking sound with his tongue against his back teeth. "I bet you can, princess."

A racket sounded in the hallway, and Roon's jovial look dropped away to be replaced by a hard glare.

"Roon," Jill called to him. "Company's arrived."

He left the room, swiping his hand in front of the doorway to engage some sort of magical shield. It flickered and ebbed with swirls like a kaleidoscope.

Belle closed her eyes and began to hum low from

the very back of her throat. She felt the vibrations as much as she heard herself. They rippled down her torso and across each limb in smooth motions. Once she had the pulsations from her larynx going in the tone she wanted, she opened her eyes and blinked a few times.

Beyond the door, Belle could still make out what was happening. There were several opponents coming from both ends of the hallway. She watched Jill punch and kick and heave herself at one of them, easily taking the upper hand so she could rip the vampire's head off. Belle was impressed, which was a rarity for her.

Belle fisted her hands at her sides, digging her nails into her palms with tension. Each time a vampire came into view, the terror that it might be Lodar ripped through her anew. Each time, her anxiety was disappointed, the fear falling away just in time for a new opponent to step up.

Rooney wasn't a slacker when it came to fighting, either. He apparently had the ability to disappear and reappear a few feet from where he'd been. The vampires, fast as they were, couldn't compensate, and he was able to use a sword-shaped wooden stake to stab them in the heart. She was mesmerized by his fluid movements, the way he jabbed and retracted his arm with smooth measure before turning to face the next foe. Her strain eased as she watched him. It wouldn't be easy for one of the Org members to get into that room with Roon, Jill, and Doc defending them.

A tiny, warm hand clutched her left fist, and she

glanced down at Nona. The littlest girl, only six, gazed up at her with wide brown eyes. "Is it gonna be okay?"

Belle dropped down to a crouch, brushing the little one's brown curls out of her eyes. She stopped humming long enough to speak. "Of course it is. I promised no one would ever hurt you again, didn't I?"

Nona's head bobbed up and down and she smiled, the little gap in her front teeth giving her a goofy but endearing look.

"Good. Now don't worry. I'll make sure nothing happens. Mr. Charlie is telling a story over there, and you don't want to miss it, do you? Lena's got a spot there for you, so hurry back over there so I can keep a close watch on things."

Without hesitation, Nona bounced back to Lena's side. The older girl glanced at Belle, seeking reassurance in her solid gaze, then turned back to hear the story. Charlie paused a moment when she began to hum again. His scraggly eyebrows bunched close together, and he reached up to rub his beard before speaking again.

Belle ignored him, turning back to the faery-protected door again and seeking comfort in the steady vibrations thumbing through her. She locked her jaw, feeling the hums in her teeth as she sought Rooney again and watched him fight off another vampire. That vampire wasn't Lodar either.

Why hadn't he come for her? She knew he wouldn't ever let her go. He'd told her she belonged to him, and he'd never relinquish his hold. With the showdown against the Org, he should be here. Her stomach tightened, and she closed her eyes to focus her breathing and humming.

She didn't even realize when the battle ended. She sensed someone close to her, and when she opened her eyes, it was the faery, standing not more than a foot away. He stared with eyes narrowed into slits, and a part of her felt like he was burrowing into her head to read her thoughts.

"You can stop that now," he told her, flicking his fingers across his throat in a gesture that she should stop the sounds she was making.

Chapter THREE

Roon watched Belle shift her weight so that she could glance behind him.

"It's over? They're gone?" she asked, confusion registering on her beautiful face.

He inflected his head in the affirmative and examined her with an intense stare. He had never met one of her kind, and in fact, he thought they were virtually extinct. But there was no denying what he'd just experienced.

When they'd finished off the last of the Org attack, Rooney looked inside this room and saw the awed expression on Charlie's face. For a moment, he wondered if one of the baddies might have skirted his wards and gotten inside, but the old man hadn't looked alarmed, just astonished.

As soon as he entered the room and made his way past her, it happened. Until that moment, he could hear Devan talking behind him to both Jill and Doc, explaining all that had occurred during their captivity. But when he crossed some invisible line, all the sounds to his rear him dulled almost into nothing and the only thing he could still hear was Belle's low humming and the children's playful chattering.

Belle had manipulated the sound waves so that all sound ahead of her was blocked. For a moment he wondered why she would do such a thing, and then when one of the little ones laughed aloud, he realized her reasoning. She was protecting the children from the sounds of the fighting going on around them. She'd used her powers to shield them from emotional harm just as surely as Roon's magical wards had shielded them from physical harm.

"They're gone." He reinforced his earlier affirmative nod. "That was impressive. How long have you been able to do that?"

She frowned, the lovely sharp brows above her eyes spiking inward. He watched the movement of her throat as she swallowed a few times, and some emotion lurched inside him. Of its own accord, his hand raised. He wanted to touch that alabaster skin of hers, but he could see the trepidation welling in her eyes.

"What business is it of yours, faery? It's no secret I'm a witch."

Rooney chuckled at her joke. Then he realized it wasn't a joke at all. He blinked as if it might clear the confusion from his mind. Surely the girl knew she wasn't merely a witch. "There must be some secret if you think you're just a witch."

It was her turn to blink. Then she raised a foot and widened her stance, lifting her chin as defiance overcame her confusion. "I don't owe you any answers or explanations about my powers."

"I think I have more answers than you do." Before he could say more, he heard his name called, and when he turned, Devvie slammed into him and put her arms around him. "Easy there," he told her, but deep down he relished the affection from the woman he'd loved for as many years as he could remember.

"You're okay? None of them hurt you? I mean, I've barely brought you to this world and you're in a fight," she fussed, brushing her hands up and down his arms and examining him with worry. From the corner of his eye, he saw Belle watching with a patronizing smirk. He winked at her, and his stomach tightened when she blushed prettily.

"Geez, Devvie." He looked away from Belle and down at Devan. "I'm not a baby. I've been in a fight before."

"Yeah," Jill piped in, walking up beside him. "You

shoulda seen him during the Games. He's the champion over there, you know."

Rooney's chest puffed out, and he raised his arm to flex his bicep for the ladies. "The champ for seventeen terms running now."

"Even champions get defeated."

His ego deflated, and he glanced at Doc with a disillusioned frown. "Damn, Doc. Did you have to go there?" When Doc and Jill had spent time in the faery realm, Doc decided to participate in a sort of exhibition water wresting match against him. Rooney would like to be able to say he'd let the vampire win, but the truth was Doc kicked his ass fair and square.

He watched Jill put her arm lovingly around Doc's waist to pull him close to her. It was hard for Roon to stay irritated with the guy when he actually liked him. Still, when Kent entered the room and his hand sought Devvie's in an affectionate clasp, he couldn't help his heavy heart. Was he destined to be the only one alone in this group?

About the time that thought crossed his mind, Belle released a deep, annoyed sigh of her own. He glanced at her and admired the way she held her head back just slightly, her chin raised only a fraction but just enough so that she had to look down at everyone around her. There was a reason he'd decided to call her princess. Her posture screamed nobility, and that glint in her eye when she looked at everyone else said, *You are only a mere peasant.*

But only to everyone except the three ragamuffins she seemed to consider her own. One of those kids—the boy, Jeremy—eased in beside her and nudged her hand, and when she gazed down at him, her face turned all soft and adoring.

"Are you and bop okay?" she asked, even the sound of her voice turning warm. The boy nodded his black head and clutched his stuffed animal tighter under his arm. He tugged her arm until she lowered herself to the child's level. Even while bent at the waist, she kept the rest of her back straight as a board and her shoulders back. "What's wrong?"

"Mr. Charlie doesn't feel so good."

At hearing those words, Rooney glanced over at the old man and saw his chest puffing in and out with heaving breathing. His face was ashen, though his cheeks were flushed bright red. He tapped Jill on the arm with the back of his hand to get her attention.

"Charlie!" his blonde friend cried as she pulled out of Doc's embrace to run to the older gentleman.

A commotion rose up as the adults hurried to tend to Charlie. Rooney stepped back and out of the way, and Belle herded the three children to her side. After everyone else filtered out of the room, he glanced over to her and smiled.

Belle cut her eyes away from him and motioned the little ones ahead of her.

"Hey, princess," he called to her, and she stopped but didn't look back. "You're not a witch. You're a siren."

Chapter
FOUR

The damned faery didn't know what he was talking about. Belle had refused to look back at him when he made his bold announcement about her powers. How could he possibly know anything about her? It was high time she got out of this crazy mess. The children were whispering about Mr. Charlie, and she knew that even though they had only been here a short time, they were fond of their elderly caretaker.

"Come along, kids," she urged, guiding them down the hallway. She could hear the other children in their ward of the hospital so she led her three in that direction. "Lena, take Jeremy and Nona to play with the other children. Then go to your room and gather your things together."

"We're leaving?" she asked, and Belle was pained to realize the girl didn't sound like she wanted to go anywhere.

"Of course we're leaving. Remember our plans? We're going to find a place all our own where no one can ever hurt us."

Glancing down at Jeremy, Lena took a deep breath and frowned. "We really like it here. Isn't this place safe enough?"

Jeremy was only a little over a year younger than Lena, though as a boy he hadn't had the same growth spurt as she'd had and was about a half foot shorter than she was. He faced Belle with serious brown eyes and nodded his head in agreement with his sister.

Internally, she cursed each of the people here at the hospital for meddling in her business and getting between her and her kids. It was true that Nicky and Gerry and the others had gotten them out from under the thumb of the Org, but she should never have let them bring her and the children to this place.

"Go on, then. Go play, and I'll be back soon."

Doubt sprouted up in the back of her mind, and she wondered if the children were right. Maybe they would be safer here. She considered Doc and Jill and all they had done for her, starting with caring for her from time to time as a child. Doc and Charlie had run this place as a clinic for the Org's magical children for a long time. When Jill came to live here, she took up a place as nursemaid as well. Burns, bumps, bruises, or sickness, this place provided solace to her and all of those magical children for years.

So why then did the thought of staying here give her an uneasy feeling? Because Lodar had found her here once, and he would come for her again. The vampire knew no bounds, and without the Bittners standing in his way, he wouldn't stop until he had her as his own.

She'd lost all ability to protect herself when Lodar or his minions were close to her. Her power of speech and use of her vocal cords failed her, and she forgot every method she had learned to defend herself. She suspected a magical spell was involved, except he was a vampire, and vampires didn't perform spells.

Padding quietly down the hallway, Belle approached the adult wing and could see by the shadows that all of the adults were in Mr. Charlie's room. This was a good time to go snooping while they were all distracted. If she had any hope of getting the children out safely, then she would need resources to live on.

A pang of guilt stabbed her heart as she considered her selfish and cold behavior. She liked the elderly doctor and always had. No matter what, she would never want to see anything bad happen to him.

She smothered her soft feelings and pressed ahead.

After going through a few rooms and bags, she finally hit the jackpot—a purse with a very fat wallet. When she opened it, she saw that this was Devan's bag. She had about four hundred dollars and change in cash plus credit cards. Also, her features were close enough to Belle's that it was possible she could use the woman's license.

Best of all, it was Devan's. That meant she didn't have to steal from her friends Jill and Doc.

Sort of your friends. Her mind waivered. She was well aware of the fact that her friends wouldn't appreciate her actions. Still, she felt a sense of loyalty to them because of all they'd done for her as a little girl and didn't want to have to take anything directly from them.

As she made her way back down the hall, she saw Rooney standing against the doorframe of Charlie's bedroom. She couldn't stop her eyes from roaming his rear top to bottom. He was wearing tight jeans that hugged his backside. It was a very nice backside.

She shook her head to force away her errant thoughts and stepped closer to hear what was going on.

"If we all go, we could get the last of the kids in no time. Charlie and Kris can stay here—" Jill spoke but was quickly interrupted by Charlie's words, though his voice was so soft she couldn't understand his words.

Belle edged even closer, near enough that she was almost touching the faery.

"C'mon, you two. It ain't nothing to get glum

about. I'm ready. These old bones are tired, you know? Besides, that little red-haired girl told me I could go now," she heard Charlie say.

"But, Charlie, we need you here. It isn't time. It isn't!" Jill insisted. "Do something."

She could just barely see into the room, but it was clear that Jill was pleading to the giant fellow, Langston.

The big man dropped his head before responding. "I cannot, my friend. Charlie and I have spoken of this. I will not interfere."

"Look at all these folks here," Charlie continued. "All of 'em with their mates. All of 'em in love…I miss my wife. Doc, you know I have to go."

Belle swallowed against a lump building in her chest. Mr. Charlie was dying. A wave of searing sadness coursed through her veins, and she wanted more than anything just to get away from the feeling. She wanted to get away from this place all together. Touching her back pocket where Devan's wallet was stuffed, she backed away and then fled down the hallway.

Chapter
FIVE

Roon wasn't used to death. It didn't happen often in the faery realm. His people could live for centuries and centuries. Time wasn't the same for them. He pushed himself back from the wall and turned away from the room. He half-expected—or hoped—to find Belle there, but all he saw was a shadow moving around the corner at the far end of the hospital.

He headed that direction and slowly peeked around the corner. There she was, leaned over and speaking in soft tones to the smallest child. Her black hair hung down across her shoulder in a glorious, thick waterfall.

Jill had told him that the woman was barely twenty, but she had a poise that was rare in a human her age. He realized his hand itched to touch those shiny locks. She handed a stuffed animal to the boy child, then lined the three of them up in a row like ducklings.

It was clear what she was up to as she glanced around a few times before guiding the kids to the exit. She was taking off with them. Rooney smiled to himself, putting a hand against the wall as he considered things.

This world was a dangerous place, especially for a gorgeous young thing like Belle. She could definitely use some faery protection. He put his hand out in front of him and waved his palm from above his head then down. His body flickered like a fluorescent light, and then his image disappeared. Grinning, he hurried off after the foursome, tailing onto the back of their group.

Rooney was a *sheoque* faery. *Sheoque* were normally stealers of children, sometimes saving an abused or neglected child by either carrying them away to the faery realm or by placing them in better circumstances in the human world. They had the ability to become invisible, to orb short distances, and to meld their minds with a child in which they were interested.

But for Roon, those abilities had been put to use a bit differently. For more than thirty years, he'd been bonded to Devvie. The Women had directed him to the special faery-witch when she was just a child. From that point until now, his sole job had been to follow her and to keep her safe, even during the years when she'd blocked their mental connection.

Devvie, he called out to her.

Hey, Rooney. Where did you go?

He watched Belle stop at the road just off the hospital property. She turned left and then right and then left again. He couldn't see her face, but he could just imagine the chagrin in her expression as she considered where to go.

I've got something I need to take care of. I may be gone a while. You know you can call if you need me, right?

Belle took Lena's hand and started walking east. He wondered if she knew how far it was to the next town.

Devvie?

Sorry, Roon. Kent was talking to me. I don't think Charlie's going to make it. I feel so horrible for Doc and Jill.

His stomach turned, and he frowned. He felt bad for his new friends, too. Bad and impotent. His people were given two wishes, one for during their lifetime and the other for their death. There was a standing tradition that most faeries used their final wish to ease their loved ones' mourning. He had no idea how to comfort someone under these circumstances.

Taking a deep breath, he licked his lips. *I'm sorry, Devvie. I know it must be tough.*

It is, she said, and he could hear the hint of

growing agitation in her voice. *Where are you? Why aren't you here?*

I'll tell you about it later. There's just something I have to do. If you need me, call me. I'll come to you, okay?

His best friend was silent a few moments. *Just be careful, Rooney. Things are different here. Don't get into any trouble.*

He snorted and smiled as he tagged onto the tail end of Belle's little entourage, who were all scurrying down the street.

It took them a couple of hours to get to town, but luckily the morning was nice—not too cool or too hot. Upon passing the sign in front of the town of Rosemary, Belle stopped and looked around. Roon stepped in front of them so he could look closely at her expression. Deep behind her eyes was uncertainty and perhaps even a bit of fear. He considered whether he should show himself and offer to help her, but he was pretty sure she'd run away from him, too.

"Are we gonna walk forever?" Jeremy asked, giving a dramatic sigh.

"No, Jeremy. Not forever. C'mon now."

She pressed on, and Lena and Jeremy both followed. Nona, however, stood rooted in place, and it took Roon a moment to realize the littlest child was looking directly at him. He glanced down at his body and found that it was still invisible. He winked to test his suspicion, and she giggled.

A souler. There was no other explanation. This child was the sort of medium who could see and commune with people through their souls. That meant even in his invisible form she could see him.

At least for a few moments. She was so young that it was likely she couldn't hold the connection with his soul for long. After a minute, she squinted and looked confused. Then she reached a hand out as if searching for him. He hopped out of her grasp just as Belle called out to her. The little girl stuck her tongue out in his direction before swirling around to catch up with her family.

Chapter SIX

A rental car made the most sense. Luckily Devan's wallet had not only her driver's license but also an insurance card. Belle used her sweetest voice when she talked to the young man at the counter. He leaned across the counter to get closer to her, his eyes mesmerized as he spoke. He was so enamored with her that there was no opportunity for him to become suspicious or even to notice that the photo on the license wasn't exactly right.

When he handed her the keys, she took a deep breath in relief and ushered the kids outside.

"Wow, our own car!" Lena exclaimed, bouncing up and down while she perused the brand new Hyundai Accent.

"It's not our car, sweetie. We're just renting it."

Jeremy gave her a thoughtful look. "Do you even know how to drive?"

Belle scoffed and motioned for him to get into the back seat of the car. "I'm an *adult*. Of course I know how to drive."

He shot her a disbelieving look before jumping into the car. Belle slipped into the driver's side and adjusted her seats. She took a few moments to move the mirrors around, checking them each three times to be sure she liked the view. Taking a deep breath, she placed both hands on the steering wheel and squeezed a couple of times.

As she eased out onto the road, it occurred to Belle that she had no earthly idea where they were going. She put a hand to her chest as it started constricting. Her breath quickened and she thought her heart might explode as it jumped into a double-time beat.

Now was not the time for a panic attack. She forced her eyes on the two-lane highway before her and focused on driving. Jeremy might not have been far off about whether she knew how to drive. It was true that, at sixteen, she had talked Trudy into teaching her how to drive a car. The pinched old woman had had a hard time refusing her requests when she used just the right tone. Still, there wasn't much call for driving when she'd moved to the Bittner house. There was a chauffeur for that sort of thing.

"I'm thirsty," Jeremy muttered after about an hour on the road. When Belle glanced back through the rearview mirror, she saw that the two girls were asleep on either side of him. He dropped his head a bit so that he was looking up at her with puppy dog eyes.

"You silly kid," she chuckled, flipping her left turn signal on so she could pull into a service station.

About as soon as the car stopped, the girls woke with wide eyes and opened both back doors, Jeremy hopping out on Lena's side.

"Hey, front and center," Belle ordered, using her most authoritative voice. All three sets of eyes turned to her, and Lena took both younger children by the hand and brought them to stand in front of her. "You can each get one drink and one snack. No sodas. Understand?"

All three heads bobbed in unison. Belle grinned and motioned with her hand and the children raced each other into the store. She followed them inside, reaching into her pocket for Devan's wallet, folding it over in her hand and clutching it to her stomach.

She kept a keen eye on the little ones and also on every other person in the station. There was a lone man in the far corner eying some magazines, a woman and her little boy waiting in line for the bathroom, and an older man at the counter scratching some lottery tickets. As her eyes skimmed the elderly fellow, they fell on a stack of spiral notebooks in a stand. Belle reached out her hand and took one, flipping the blank pages.

When the older man slapped his hand on the counter, she jumped and closed her eyes. He fussed a moment about his losing ticket then shuffled away. Belle stepped forward and placed the notepad on the counter, clucking at the kids to come along. They each placed their drinks and their snacks beside the notepad.

She handed the cashier a few bills and requested a receipt when he didn't offer her one. He squinted his eyes at her but handed her the slip of paper anyway. When she slipped her change into the wallet, a card fell out. It was for a vacation place in Danville, Arkansas. A clever grin cut across her face. Now they had a destination.

Nona hopped into the car as soon as the doors were open, and Belle could hear her giggling to herself. It seemed the youngest of the children was always able to entertain herself. Jeremy and Lena were arguing over who got to sit directly behind the driver's seat; for what reason, Belle had no idea.

Fighting over the middle seat would have made more sense, but Nona already had that one so she figured the older kids just wanted to fuss about something. She ignored them for the moment and focused on carefully writing down the money she had spent so far. She might not be above stealing a wallet to protect herself and her kids, but she damn sure wasn't going to take complete advantage. She fully intended to find a way to pay Devan back every penny.

"You need any help, babe?"

Belle didn't recognize the voice, but it sent a shiver up her spine. She swallowed and turned to face a tall and burly man with shaggy dark hair and a five-o'clock shadow. He had beady black eyes that skimmed up and down her body. His lascivious grin gave her the creeps.

If that weren't enough, he was also a werewolf. She scanned the area for others, but everyone else in the vicinity appeared to be human. *Where's Lodar?* her mind screamed.

The werewolf took a few steps closer, and Belle sucked in a breath. Her cheeks burned as her blood pounded in her ears. If she could hear the panicked beating of her heart then surely he could as well with his wolf ears. He put a hand on the car, blocking off any exit in that direction. Terror choked off her ability to speak so she just backed away from him, bumping hard into the driver's side door of the car.

Chapter SEVEN

Rooney waited in the front passenger seat while Belle and the kids went inside the service station. He had dozed for most of the trip, and his eyes still felt heavy with the kind of grogginess from a long daytime nap.

Little Nona was the first to get back into the car, and when he swiveled in his seat to look at her, he could immediately tell by the glint in her eyes that she could see him again. In response, he stuck his tongue out at her. She mimicked him, sticking hers out, too.

Rooney laughed and shook his head. She was a

precocious kid, and looking into her glittering eyes made him want to entertain her all the more. He curled his tongue, blowing air through it and making a little whistle sound. She frowned and manipulated her tongue, trying and failing to imitate his movements.

He forced his tongue out even farther. Then he slowly flipped it upside down. That's when Nona's eyes widened, and she giggled, curling her legs and arms close to her body in mirth. He was in the process of crossing his eyes and quirking his mouth into a goofy grin when they felt a thump against the vehicle.

Nona hopped up onto her knees, and Rooney swung around to see Belle. Her back was plastered against the vehicle and her hands were up in front of her. A burly guy was pressing close to her, and by the movement of his nose, Roon could only guess he was sniffing at her.

He figured it was a werewolf, but that was just a guess. The truth was he'd never met one face-to-face. There weren't any in the faery realm, although he wasn't really sure why.

Rooney lifted his left leg and worked his way from the passenger seat to the driver's seat before getting out of the car. There were a lot of people around. Otherwise he would have kept his invisibility cloak so he could sneak up on the baddie. Instead, he waved his hand to reappear then exited the car.

"Hey," he called out to the werewolf. "I don't think she's interested."

The were flicked his gaze up at him and narrowed his eyes. Belle gasped and looked back at Roon, her expression showing both astonishment and relief. She flinched when the guy clamped his hand around her arm. Rooney stepped closer.

"And who the hell do you think you are?" the wolf snarled.

Not responding, Roon took several more steps until he was standing on their side of the car, just a few feet away from them.

"My brother. He's my brother, and we're in a hurry. You understand, don't you? We have a long way to go, and we need to get moving. Okay?"

Her voice was angelic, soft, and smooth. Her eyes were looking right at the werewolf, drawing him into a trance. He leaned toward her, but not in a threatening way. He was weaving on his feet, front and back. After a few seconds, his hand released its hold on her, his fingers slipping loose and his arm falling to his side as if through water.

"Let's go, Belle."

It was Jeremy's voice. Rooney had forgotten they were there, but when he looked, three sets of wide eyes were watching the were's every move.

"Get in the car, children." Belle's words were said in a calm, even tone, though she didn't take her gaze off her attacker. She reached a hand up to rub the red finger marks on her upper arm as she backed to the passenger side of the car and opened the door. "You too, faery.

Get in the car."

The authority in her voice left no room for argument, though Roon had a very good argument to make. Still, he did as she said and opened the door, getting into the driver's side. When all the doors were closed, Belle hit a button and locked them. She reached out her hand and dangled the keys out to him, still keeping an eye on the bewitched werewolf.

When he didn't take the keys from her, she finally broke her gaze and turned to him. "What are you waiting for? It won't hold for long. We need to get out of here."

Rooney opened his mouth to speak but closed it again. His cheeks burned with embarrassment, and he turned away from her so she wouldn't see. He glanced out the window at the people milling about the service station, fueling their cars, or munching on snacks.

The truth was, he had no idea how to drive a car.

Swinging his hand out, he clasped the key ring and slipped the key into the ignition. He wasn't sure he had the nerve to tell Belle the real story behind his hesitation, so with a deep breath, he turned the ignition. A surge of excitement rushed through his veins when the vehicle roared to life.

Belle got involved with the children again, urging them to buckle their seatbelts, chiding them not to spill their snacks. He took the moment to glance down at the controls. He had "seen" Devan drive many times in the years he'd been secretly watching over her. In fact, he had even watched her attend driver's ed class. He figured this couldn't be all that hard.

With a determined expression, he reached down and pressed the button on the gear shift, but it wouldn't move. He racked his brain to recall Devvie's lessons and finally remembered something about the brake. Contorting his head to the side, he looked down at the two pedals near his feet.

He lifted his right foot onto the ball and moved the foot left and right over the two pedals, squinting to remember which one was which. He closed his eyes to get a mental image before he grinned and placed his toes on the brake. At that moment, he felt the gear shift loosen as he slipped it into the first position, the one marked "R."

A bit at a time he pulled his foot off the brake. When the car started back, he jammed his foot back down and the car slammed to a halt. Belle gave him a queer look then went back to punching something into a little handheld device.

After a few tries, he managed to back the car out of the parking space and get it to the exit of the service station lot. He gazed left then right at the busy street in front of him, wondering which way to go.

"Here," Belle told him, placing the device on the dashboard and flicking her hand at him dismissively. "Follow that."

When he looked, he saw it was a GPS unit, and the female voice told him to turn left. He waited for traffic to clear before pulling out onto the highway with some trepidation. After a few moments, he started to loosen up, grinning to himself for successfully learning to drive a car. *Maybe there are some things we are missing out on in the faery world,* he thought to himself.

Chapter
EIGHT

If she didn't know any better, she would have thought the faery didn't know how to drive a car. Still, after a few moments, he managed to get them on the road again, this time heading for Danville, Arkansas.

It took her a while to get over the initial burst of emotion brought on by the werewolf. It was hard to believe it was just a fluke encounter, but she felt certain she would have known if Lodar had been in the vicinity. She was sure he hadn't been. He was a vampire, so he couldn't have been out in the daytime, but he had a special van he liked to use—one that blocked all rays of sunlight so he could travel and direct his underlings.

Still, if she didn't put some distance between them and the hospital, she was just as sure he'd track her down.

She side-eyed the red-haired man driving the car and huffed a frustrated sigh. "What the hell are you doing here anyway?"

He glanced at her and grinned. "That's no way to talk to the guy who just saved your ass."

Belle snorted and crossed her arms over her chest. "You did no such thing. I'm quite certain I saved my own...self."

"Sure, whatever you say, princess. But if you could save yourself so easily, why'd you take so long doing it?"

"She gets a ball in her throat sometimes. It makes her not be able to breathe right."

Belle didn't turn around to look at Jeremy, though she saw Rooney looking at him through the rearview mirror. When she felt the faery's eyes on her again, she sniffed and turned toward the window.

"A ball in your throat, eh? Well, that explains a lot. So that fellow, he was a werewolf, right?"

She hesitated before nodding. She didn't even like the man, but he had a way of making her want to engage in conversation with him. "Yes, a werewolf. That's why I was caught off guard. I thought he might not be alone."

"Yeah, thought the pack might be with him." Rooney nodded, understanding.

Only he didn't really understand. It wasn't the wolf's pack that had had her worried—it was Lodar. He liked to use wolves for his lackeys. Werewolves weren't especially ambitious, so working with them presented no issues to Lodar's drive to advance in the Org's upper echelon. Weres could also be depended upon to work for a stipend—a cheap stipend invariably.

"Are you going to answer my question?" She turned back to Rooney. "I want know what you're doing here. Did you follow us all this way?"

"He rided with us. He sitted right there," Nona piped in from the back seat, pointing to where Belle was sitting.

"Hey, snitch, are you giving away my secrets?" he asked the little girl with an exaggerated angry glare. After a moment, he winked and stuck his tongue out at her through the mirror. Nona laughed with glee.

"He rode with us," Belle said, correcting the young one's grammar. "And he sat right here." She paused and glanced at the faery, looking him up and down. She intended the look to be an assessment of his magical abilities, but before she knew it, she was noticing the definition of muscle in his arms, the flatness of his stomach underneath his t-shirt, the thick strength of his thighs inside his jeans.

"Ahem."

When he cleared his throat, she had the urge to

clear hers, too. Her mouth felt dry, and it took her all of about thirty seconds to realize her mouth was hanging open. She popped her jaw closed and glared at him, but the knowing look on his face had her cheeks flaming with embarrassment.

"Like what you see, princess?" He spoke barely above a whisper so that the children couldn't hear him. Heat pooled in her chest, radiating through her body and making her limbs feel weak.

"I like that I *can* see you," she retorted, letting anger bubble up to cover the other things she was feeling but didn't want to think about. "Don't do that again. If you're going to make a pest of yourself, then the least you can do is stay visible."

"You're gorgeous, you know that? Especially when you're pissed."

Her eyes widened at his words. Before she could help herself, her gaze was drawn to his lips, the corner lifting in a wry smile.

"I don't like you," Belle told him, hissing the words.

"Yeah, you do. If you didn't, you wouldn't be letting me drive you and those kiddos to wherever it is we're going. Nah, if you didn't like me, you'd use that siren's croon of yours to get me to pull over and get out of this car."

"Just shut up and drive."

His laughter echoed in the small vehicle, and the kids giggled right along with him. Belle had to grit her teeth together to keep from smiling. The damned faery was getting to her, and that was the last thing she needed.

Chapter
NINE

Rooney cocked his head left and right to pop his stiff neck. He'd been driving for about three hours straight, and his body was starting to protest. He wasn't used to sitting in one place for so long. Belle had offered several times to take over—albeit a little stiffly—but he had refused. He could see how exhausted she was, and about an hour earlier, she had finally leaned her head against the door and gone to sleep.

"Beetle bug green." Lena pointed to the round-topped car as it passed them.

"Dang," Jeremy pouted. "You're three ahead now."

Lena grinned smugly and continued glaring out the window. It had taken Roon a few times before he realized what game the kids were playing. Not only had he never driven before, he wasn't exactly up on his knowledge of vehicle makes and models.

Glancing into the rearview mirror, he saw Nona intently swishing a crayon back and forth in her coloring book. She was chewing on her upper lip as she focused on her work.

Just then, Jeremy jumped and leaned against her, shoving her arm and gesticulating. "Beetle bug yellow, Beetle bug green, Beetle bug blue, and Beetle bug black!" he exclaimed to Lena.

Rooney watched as an eighteen-wheeler passed with all brand new Beetles on its trailer. When he glanced back in the mirror, he saw Lena's mouth drop open in astonishment. "No fair!"

"Na, na, na, nana!"

"You messed me up!" Nona cried, tears welling in her eyes as she clutched her picture to her chest and shoved Jeremy away from her.

All the commotion woke Belle up. She rubbed at her eyes and then turned around to face the children. "What's going on? Jeremy, get back into your seat."

All three young ones tried to explain their sides of

the story at once. Rooney frowned, shook his head, and then yawned. "Why don't we pull over up ahead?" he asked Belle. "There's a rest stop, and the kids could probably use a little running around."

Sleep was still in her expression, and it made her even lovelier. As much as that, her guard was down just the tiniest bit, so when he looked at her, she really let him see more of the secret emotions she held deep inside. He dived into her eyes, caressing her with his gaze. After a few moments, her eyelashes fluttered, and she cast her eyes down with a nod. "A rest would be good for them."

Lena and Jeremy jumped at the chance to stretch their legs, bouncing out of the car with such exuberance that Belle had to run to catch up to them. Rooney could hear her telling them exactly how far they could venture, what they could do, and what they could not. The girl had more orders than a drill sergeant.

Stepping out onto the leaf covered grass, Roon reached both arms up and stretched, moaning and groaning as he twisted this way and that. He bent over at the waist and looked into the back seat at Nona. She was frowning, her lower lip puckered out and her coloring book still tight against her chest. There were streaks on her face from her tears. He figured the little one was tired as much as anything. A long trip like this could be trying to anyone.

"C'mon out, cutie. You need to walk around, or those legs of yours will shrivel up."

She cut him a glare but didn't move.

"You don't believe me? I've seen it. Old Timmy Turfunkle. That dude decided to read *War and Peace* one time. Only Turfunkle can't read very well. Took him five years! All that time, sitting there reading…when he finally finished, he tried to stand, and his legs were two feet shorter than they had been before. Had to walk like this…" To demonstrate, Roon dropped into a squat and waddled around.

Nona was giggling before he finished the story, but by the time he started squat-walking, she was laughing aloud. He stood and reached out his hand for her, and she took it, crawling out of the car and into the cool late afternoon air.

"Getting chilly, don't you think?" He glanced down at her for an answer, but she shook her head, still smiling.

When he cast his eyes back up, he saw Belle approaching. He took Nona by both arms and swung her away from him so she could run along. His lovely companion shot him a small smile as she passed him on her way to the car.

He watched her lean into the back seat, collecting the children's trash from the floorboard to clean things up. Her very shapely backside wiggled to and fro, and he found himself wondering just how thin those jeans over her really were and whether he could feel the heat of her skin if he placed his hand on her derriere. She glanced at him over her shoulder, looking almost as if she knew his thoughts.

Rooney waggled his eyebrow at her before turning to face the children. As he walked along, shuffling leaves, he called out to Devvie in his mind.

Hey, sexy. What's going on?

He chuckled as he watched Lena pick up a handful of leaves and toss them at Jeremy, who was wielding a stick as if it were a sword. Nona stood on the sidelines, egging her pseudo-sister on.

Rooney, you've been quiet a long while. Everything okay?

Course it is, he told her, closing his eyes so he could see her. He recognized her surroundings well. She was back at her father's estate, going through files at the big desk that had at one time been the old man's.

All of her childhood, he had watched over her in that house, her constant companion until her teens when therapy encouraged her to lock him out. When he finally broke through to her again all those months ago and reconnected, he'd been ecstatic. He finally saw his chance to make his love for her known.

The Women had told him that wasn't possible, but Roon didn't want to believe it. Not until that kiss. That damnable, wonderful, awful kiss when he finally got to taste her. That kiss when he finally knew she would never be in love with him.

He telepathically continued contact with Devan even after she'd made it clear she couldn't have feelings for him. Still, once her relationship with Kent had really heated up, he stopped "looking" in on her. It hurt too much to watch her get touchy-feely with someone else.

Now Roon mentally searched the room for Devvie's lover, Kent, but didn't see him anywhere.

If you say so, Devan said, looking up from some papers and staring off into space. He watched the little dent she got between her eyebrows pop up as she frowned. After a second, she started chewing the inside of her mouth.

Stop worrying. I'm good. I like it so much here in your world that maybe I'll just stay. So how's lover boy? Been gettin' any lately?

She rolled her eyes and huffed. *Sicko!*

Rooney opened one eye and looked back at Belle. She'd finished rummaging through the car and was now carrying an armload of empty drink containers and wrappers to the waste can. Her dark eyes met his, and she hesitated mid-step as she locked onto his gaze.

I could dive into those eyes and never have to come up for air.

Roon! Devvie protested. *Friendly flirting is all right. Love words are not.*

Rooney shook his head and chuckled. He hadn't realized he was thinking the words aloud for Devan to hear. He most certainly wasn't talking about her, but she couldn't know that.

Yeah, Devvie. I know. Listen, I won't keep you. I just wanted to check in and make sure you were okay.

I'd call you if I wasn't. You'd call me, right? If you need help, you'll let me know?

He needed help all right, but it wasn't the kind Devan could give him.

Chapter
TEN

Belle could feel Rooney's eyes searing into her even without looking. She'd been ogled by men before so it was something she was used to. When she'd reached puberty and started to come into her magic, she became eye-candy to their visitors instead of a supplicant for her vampire parents.

Still, there was something different about the way Rooney looked at her. His look made tingles of excitement race through her limbs. When he looked at her, she wanted to move closer to him, not run away.

Arms laden with the children's trash, Belle walked

toward the waste can beside a tree at the rest stop. About halfway there, she made the mistake of meeting Roon's gaze. Her steps halted immediately, and her breath caught in her throat.

He stared, his eyes caressing her in a way that was erotic and sensual and made her want his hands on her too.

Belle shook her head to clear the thoughts that were so unlike her. Warmth crept into her cheeks as she forced her eyes away from him and moved to throw the garbage into the can. He approached her, but she refused to look at him, instead brushing her hands on her hips and turning 180 degrees in the opposite direction to check on the kids.

"They seem to be having a pretty good time," Rooney spoke, stopping beside her. From the corner of her eye, she saw him slip his hands into his pockets.

"They're really good kids. Hardly ever cause a bit of trouble."

He nodded and smiled down at her.

"Really. They don't argue like that very often. It's been a trying series of weeks."

"So, they aren't siblings, right?"

She took a deep breath to ease the tension in her chest. This conversation was innocuous and there was no reason to be uptight with him when he'd been nice to them. "Lena and Jeremy are. Jeremy was only about Nona's age when they came to live with the Bittners." She cut a glance at him, frowning. "I guess you know what I mean by that?"

Rooney slipped a hand out of his jeans and rubbed it across his jaw a few times, huffing air through his fingers. "I know about the Org, Belle. I know they deal in selling magical kids to vampires."

The disgust in his voice jabbed at her. Vampires could strengthen their powers and increase their lives by feeding on anyone with magical blood. But the energy within a magical child's blood was undiluted and potent. The Org was in the business of selling those children as supplicants for vampires

Most of the time Belle tried to bury the truth of her life and her childhood in some little hole at the back of her mind. It wasn't an easy thing to do, but it was the only way to survive without going crazy. It was harder to ignore the fact that the truth of her life was now the truth of Lena's, Jeremy's, and Nona's lives, too.

She inhaled a shaky breath before continuing. "Lena was getting older, and it was Mrs. Bittner's idea to look for a new child. That was about six months ago. Nona's just a baby really, and she keeps to herself a lot. Internalizes."

He was looking at her again and she felt open and raw. He seemed to understand what she was saying, and the emotions under the surface were threatening to overcome her.

"But she's a souler. She's had spirits with her most of her life, so she isn't really alone." he finally said.

"She's special," Belle acknowledged, nodding to

emphasize her agreement with his words.

"You were alone, though. There was no one there for you when you were her age, was there?"

Just when she thought it was safe, that she'd had her emotions under control, he stripped away all of her protections. She swallowed a sob, the sound spilling from her lips like a hiss. She wrung her hands together, then slid her fingers up to her arms to cross them over her chest. "I was the only child, yes. I was late to come into my powers compared to most magical kids, I'm told."

She could see her own chest rising and falling as her breath came in quick gasps. He wasn't looking at her now. Instead, he had his face turned towards the children. Belle clenched her eyes closed until she could see stars. When she felt Rooney touch her arm and slip his hand under hers, she didn't pull away. Rather, she tightened her fingers around his and held on like her life depended on it.

"Belle, you aren't alone right now," he told her in a firm voice.

When she opened her eyes, she saw that he still wasn't looking at her. It was as if he knew the meeting of their eyes would be her complete undoing. She appreciated his restraint more than he could ever realize.

Her gaze cut down to the place where their hands were still connected. Swallowing down the bare emotions she felt, she tugged her hand away from his and took a few steps in the direction of the children. Rooney made no move to stop her, to hold her, or to follow her.

A few moments later they corralled the children and ushered them all back into the vehicle. Roon tossed her the keys, and she took them with a nod, her silent agreement that it was her turn to drive.

"When are we gonna eat?" Jeremy whined nearly the moment Belle pulled out onto the highway.

Rooney snorted a chuckle and rolled his head to the side to look at her. "Your call, princess. You've got the wheel."

Her stomach rumbled its concurrence that it was time for sustenance so she glanced into the rearview mirror at the kids.

"All right. Let's see what the signs say as we get to the next town."

Lena moved her head up and down with enthusiasm, Jeremy cried, "Woohoo," and little Nona smiled as she placed a finger into her mouth. Belle watched Rooney pivot in his seat and use two fingers to pull the corners of his lips wide with a growl. All three children hooted with contagious laughter even Belle couldn't contain.

After an unhealthy meal of burgers, fries, and sodas, something Belle would never have fed the kids normally, they got back on the road. Lena, Jeremy, and Nona all passed out within about thirty minutes, Rooney in just over forty-five. The hum of the tires against the pavement soothed her, though she didn't feel tired.

Not tired at all, in fact. She was alive. She was free. She was on her way to a new life, and even the boring drive in a silent car couldn't tamp her enthusiasm. She side-eyed her companion to the right. He wasn't part of her original plan, but somehow she no longer minded.

Roon looked different in sleep. The lines on his face were softened, although there were permanent indentations at the corners of his lips—evidence of his ever-ready smile. All flirtation was gone now, leaving something deeper exposed. That something was still charismatic and youthful. He looked charming and very attractive.

It took her a moment to affirm to herself that she was attracted to him. His hand on her arm earlier left her tingling for more of his touch. She wanted to touch him, to put her hands on him. She tightened her fingers on the steering wheel and sighed.

Maybe having him with her would give them more security. He obviously knew how to fight, so if Lodar or his people found her, he could help protect them. And he was a faery. If Lodar found them and they needed to get away, all Roon had to do was open one of his magic portals.

Yes, having him along was a very good addition to her plan.

With a grin, she reached over and switched on the radio, quickly turning the volume down to a level that wouldn't be likely to disturb her occupants. Tapping her thumbs on the steering wheel, she grooved along to the beat of the music and drove and drove and drove.

Chapter
ELEVEN

Sleep was still a hazy veil over his mind when Rooney felt a butterfly touch against his cheek. He knew it was Belle even without seeing her. She charged the very air around her, and the effect was palpable. He swallowed, sucking in a forceful breath through his nose. He felt Belle withdraw her fingers with a tiny gasp, and a grin tugged at the corners of his lips.

"Morning..." he muttered, opening one eye to look around. It was still dark out, so he wondered what time of the day it really was. "Or is it?"

"It is." She nodded, sitting up straight and putting

on her aloof face. "Just after five actually. The sign says the office opens at seven."

Rooney took a look around with both eyes. He could see the rosy hue of dawn along the horizon with the black shadows of pine trees looming against the backdrop. Wherever they were, it was heavily wooded and probably secluded. This was the sort of environment he was used to at his home in the faery realm.

When he circled his eyes around, his gaze finally came upon a small log cabin just in front of their car. In the background, he saw other cabins a good ways from them. It didn't take his mind long to recognize his surroundings, and when he did, a spike of alarm shot through his body and he turned suddenly, grabbing Belle's hand in a strong grip before she could open the door.

"What did you do?"

"Let go of me," she hissed, fisting her hand and trying to pull away.

He knew this place from watching Devvie. She owned all of it, and this was where, just months earlier, she had discovered the extent of her powers and killed off some of the Org higher-ups.

It was true that those Org members, Adriel and a few others, knew about this place, but all of them, with the exception of the warlock, Robbie, were dead. And Robbie was banished to the faery realm, so it was unlikely there was any way he could have communicated the location to anyone else.

No, there was no easy explanation for how Belle could have taken them here. She certainly wasn't chummy with anyone at the hospital.

"How did we get here, Belle? What the hell did you do?"

She shook her head, her mouth open in an astonishment.

"Belle, I'm not gonna ask again. How the hell did you find this place?"

"Belle?" Nona's voice rose in a hoarse whisper from the back seat.

Rooney glanced at the little girl's drowsy eyes and then back at Belle. Groaning, he released her hand with a shove then exited the car. He heard her open the driver's side door, and he closed his eyes, inhaling a breath to orb to the spot beside her. She gasped and recoiled, but he took her wrists, shoved her from the door, and kicked it closed with his foot. With his lips just a millimeter from hers, he opened his mouth and said, "Tell me."

"A card. It was a c-card," she stuttered, her voice just a whisper. "In her wallet."

"Devvie's wallet." It wasn't a question, but a statement. "You stole her wallet. It's her money you've been using to pay for this. This car, the gas, the food. You were going to use it to pay for a cottage here."

He watched Belle's throat convulse as she swallowed. "Yes."

"Bitch." The word was full of vitriol but spoken in a murmur because by that time the back driver's door had opened and he could feel one of the children watching them.

When he backed away from her, Belle ran a shaking hand through her hair before turning to Jeremy, who was standing beside her. He watched her touch him on his head and crouch low with a plastic smile.

"Hey, there. Did you get a good night's sleep?"

He nodded, clutching his bop against his chest, looking small and fragile. Nona shuffled out of the car next, rubbing her eyes, and kicked through the leaves toward the cabin. Roon peeked inside and saw that Lena's little body was curled up against the far back door, still asleep.

"Do they gots beds? I'm still sleepy," Nona said, looking at Rooney expectantly.

Rooney chewed on what was happening while Belle saw to the kids, ushering them off into the woods to do their "business." The Danville property wasn't exactly a closely guarded secret, but showing up here had been enough of a surprise to throw him off. When he'd asked Belle and she got that guilt-laden, panicked look in her eyes, he knew very well he'd hit on something wrong.

She'd stolen Devvie's wallet. She'd cheated his life-long friend, the woman he loved.

He should have been furious about that, but instead he wanted to protect Belle. He wanted to shield her from Devan's displeasure and Kent's fury—because Kent would surely be angry. It made no sense to him, but instead of instantly snatching the wallet away from her so he could return it to Devvie, his mind was circling with reasons and excuses for her.

And his dilemma pissed him off much more than her actions in and of themselves.

Because on top of it all, what he really wanted to do was grab her at the wrists again, shove her against the car hood, and kiss her breathless.

He closed his eyes and focused in on Devan.

You awake? he asked her. It was a silly question because he knew she was. He could see her there in the chair beside the bed where Kent was sleeping. There was a spot of mussed covers beside the blond man, and it was clear she had just gotten out of that bed. The bed where she had slept and probably made love with him.

He thought it would bother him to see her there, but somehow it didn't. Devvie tilted her head towards the ceiling and glanced up into space at the sound of his voice. She was in the process of braiding her long brown hair. *Hey you. I'm awake. And you probably knew that, too.*

Yeah, I knew. Listen, I need some help. He watched her lean forward and sit up straighter. *Just relax, Devvie. Nothing's wrong.*

Well, you're starting to freak me out, you know? You're acting weird.

Rooney shook his head and chuckled, opening one

eye to make sure Belle and the kids weren't approaching. *You worry too much. But I'm sorry I'm acting weird.* He hesitated a moment before spilling the truth, taking a deep breath. He wondered why it was so hard to tell her who he was with. And better yet, why he was with her.

What is it, Roon? What's going on with you?

It's Belle. That chick from the hospital.

Jill and Doc's old patient. The girl with the lungs on her?

He laughed despite himself. When Nicky and Gerry first found Belle and the kids and brought them to the hospital, there was an incident where Belle had screamed so loud, she nearly tore the rafters off the building. No one suspected at that time that she was a siren, but then sirens weren't supposed to exist anymore, either.

Yeah, she's got one great set of lungs.

Devan rolled her eyes and stood up from her seat, tossing her heavy braid over her shoulder. *Pfft! Those weren't the lungs I was talking about, you sicko.*

He laughed again, pleased he could still get a rise out of her. *So anyway, I followed her and the kids. They're on the run, afraid of something, I think. We're in Danville…*

Chapter
TWELVE

Rooney carried the still-sleeping Lena into their cabin. Belle waited for him to get inside before she closed the door. Just as he was making his way into one of the little bedrooms, Lena stirred and woke up. He set the girl on her feet and then changed directions to head into the bathroom. Belle inhaled and exhaled a long held breath.

She wasn't sure how he'd gotten them a cabin. He insisted she wait outside while he went in to see the overseer, and he didn't ask for the wallet, a credit card, or anything. Maybe faeries carried human money.

Maybe they had a way to fabricate it. Either way, he'd gotten them a nice place to stay.

It was clearly intended for a family as there was a booster seat and a highchair against the bar near the kitchen. Also, outside the back windows, she saw several tire swings swaying in the breeze.

"Do we all get our own room?" Jeremy asked, looking up at her with expectant, wide eyes.

"Uhm…" Belle moved to the open doors on the far side of the cabin. "Looks like no. There are two bedrooms. You kids get one, I get the other."

"Where's Roon gonna sleep?"

It was Nona who asked, but Belle couldn't bring herself to turn and look at the girl just yet. Her cheeks were burning with a hot blush. She wasn't sure what had come over her, but the moment Nona had asked the question, a sudden answer popped into her mind. She knew just where she wanted Rooney to sleep, and that was in the very bedroom she was looking at. The one sans bunk beds—only a single king.

That was when the object of her thoughts stepped out of the bathroom and walked behind her. He leaned in close to her ear, his nearness rustling her hair. "We need to talk, princess."

Belle swallowed and nodded as she turned to the kids.

"Can I trust you kiddos to stay right in the back and play on the tires?"

"Swings!" Nona screeched when she noticed them

through the window. She sailed for the back door of the cabin, Jeremy on her heels.

"Lena, will you keep an eye on them?"

Lena yawned. "Yes, ma'am."

Once the children were outside the house, Belle rolled back her shoulders and lifted her chin to meet Rooney's gaze full-on. It took a good deal of effort to keep her face impassive as she lowered herself into a seat and calmly crossed her ankles. "Yes?"

"Geez, maybe I should call you the ice queen instead of princess. You're a cold one when you want to be. Don't give me that aloof look. You're lucky your ass didn't get arrested."

"I don't know what you're talking about. I've been very careful."

Rooney took several long strides across the room until he was standing in front of her. He peered down, his green eyes sparking. "Devan owns this place, princess. She owns every acre of this place, and as soon as you tried to pass one of her cards to the overseer, he would've busted you."

She felt the blood drain from her face. Her tight expression faltered, though she refused to break eye contact with him. "What are you going to do?" she whispered.

He didn't speak. He just held out his hand to her. She knew exactly what that meant. She licked her lips before glancing down and reaching into her pocket for the wallet. Once in his palm, he curled his fingers around it then turned away from her.

"What are you going to do?" she repeated, standing up and wringing her hands.

He stopped and stood rigid for a moment. "I'm going to return this to Devvie."

Her stomach lurched, and she felt that old fear and anxiety of the unknown work its way into her mindset again. He was leaving them. She was going to be on her own again.

It shouldn't have hurt as much as it did. She barely knew this man. Sure, he'd flirted with her, he'd come along on a long drive with them, he'd even offered her a bit of comfort. But what did any of that mean? He was just another person she couldn't depend on. She and the kids only had themselves.

No, her mind insisted. She couldn't do this alone. This very incident was proof enough of that. She was naïve, she was young, and she didn't know anything about the real world. Yes, it was horrifying to be a magical child sold into bondage to vampire parents. Certainly the prospect of Lodar finding them and getting to her set her blood ice-cold with fear.

Despite all of that, the outside world on her own was truly the most terrifying prospect.

"I want you to stay," she heard herself call out to him. "Please."

When she spoke, his entire body shifted. His tension melted away, and she saw his shoulders lower just a bit. He took a deep breath and turned to face her.

"Don't do that. Don't try to ply me with your siren's call. I'm coming back."

His dark green eyes bored into her and caressed her inside and out. She reached up to brush away a strand of hair before she moved her head up and down. "Okay. That's good."

He kept staring at her until she felt uncomfortable and forced her eyes away. She glanced out the window and saw Jeremy chasing Lena, while Nona was swinging back and forth on one of the tire swings. When she turned back, she was startled to find Rooney directly in front of her. He was so close she could feel the warmth of his breath on her cheek.

Her heart palpitated in her chest, and she was sure there was nothing he could have done to startle her any more than orbing to the spot right before her. She opened her mouth to scold him, something she often did when thrown off-guard. Rooney took that moment to swoop his lips down onto hers. With her lips already open, all he had to do was delve his tongue inside to stroke hers.

Belle moaned and melted against him. He curled one arm around her waist and pulled her up tight against his body. Her fingers clasped at his chest, reveling in the hard tone of muscle under her hands. Every nerve in her burned with need even as he deepened the kiss, leaning into her so that her entire upper body bent back.

She wasn't complaining. She was holding on for all

she had. She was pretty sure her body was about to fuse with his when he pulled his mouth away from hers, pecking her once more on her swollen lips.

"Let me make something clear to you, princess." He spoke against her lips, his voice rough and low. "I'd do anything for Devvie. She's my best friend. I'm going to return this wallet to her. I'm not going to say a damn thing about your little thievery, and then I'm going to come back here." He held his hand out in front of her, fingers splayed. Instinctively, she put her own hand up and touched each of her fingers and her thumb to his. "And you and I are going to have a long talk."

As soon as their fingers met, a spark tingled through her hand, growing and sending a warmth straight through to a place deep in her mind. It jolted her, and when she looked into his eyes, she felt like she was seeing more of him in some way. She knew he was waiting for her to acknowledge what he'd said, but it was hard to develop a full thought in that moment. "Okay," was all she could manage to breathe.

Chapter
THIRTEEN

Rooney opened the golden door into the courtyard of the hospital and stepped through. No one was around, which was a relief. He needed to get himself under control. His entire body throbbed with desire in the aftermath of that kiss. He glanced down at his crotch and took a deep breath. A certain part of his body in particular was throbbing.

Damn, the woman turned him on. When his lips met hers, he'd fully expected her to recoil and smack him. Not that he thought she wasn't attracted to him. He knew good and well that she was. He just didn't think her stoic façade would crumble so quickly.

It hadn't just crumbled; it had evaporated the instant their mouths met. When she'd grabbed at his body and held on to him, contouring her form to his, it took all his control to tear himself away from her.

Now, he reached up and combed his hand through his red hair, scratching and ruffling the spiky locks. "Get it together, Roon," he hissed to himself.

"Hello, my friend."

It was Langston. He would know the giant's soothing voice anywhere. Rooney didn't really know Langston, having only met him briefly, but he had watched Devvie's interaction with him enough times. The shaman had a calming effect on people, and Roon was no more immune to it than anyone else.

"Hey there, big guy." Roon took a deep breath and smiled. "How's it hanging?"

Langston grinned big and nodded as if he knew some secret. "All is well here. Devan has been concerned. She feared you could not take care of yourself in this great big world."

He snorted and shook his head. "She can smother a man."

"Indeed. And you, my friend, are in luck. Because Kent is with Doc at the moment, so Devan has some privacy in which to talk. That is why you are here, is it not?"

Damn, the man had a way of knowing things. It was true he wanted to talk to his friend, but first things first. He finished the pleasantries, then bounded into the hospital through the door closest to the room he knew Devan was sharing with Kent. He found her purse there on the floor and tucked the wallet inside on the bottom.

With any luck, she hadn't even noticed it was missing yet. Of course, he'd eventually have to tell her since the charges Belle had made to her credit cards would show up, but he wanted things to be settled between him and Belle before that took place.

He jerked his hand out of the bag just as he heard footsteps coming down the hallway. Guilt painted his face hot, but he managed to purse his lips and let out a little whistle as he stepped through the doorway. "Devvie? That you coming?"

It wasn't. It was one of the little ones, a cherubic girl he remembered was named Chelsea. She grinned and stared up at him with wide eyes. "'Lo, Mr. Rooney."

Roon laughed and ruffled the curls on top of her head. "No *mister* Rooney. Just call me Roon. Do you know where Devan is?"

The girl's head bobbed up and down and she pointed in the direction from which she'd come. "She's in the kitchen. I had a accident."

"You did? What happened?" he asked, adding an extra dose of drama to his voice.

"Spilled my juice." And she clutched his arm so she could hold out her leg to show him the bright purple stain on the bottom of her britches.

"Grape juice?"

"Yum!" She smiled again, nodding.

"Rooney!" Devvie's voice was raised in jubilation, and he gazed up to look into her radiant brown-gold eyes.

"Hey there, sexy."

She rolled those eyes but laughed. "Can you change your clothes by yourself, Chelsea?"

"Yes, ma'am," the little one replied before bounding away down the hall towards the children's rooms.

"So..." Devan slapped him on the arm with a knowing smile. "Tore yourself away from the troublemaker long enough to come say hello?"

"Troublemaker?" he queried innocently as he followed her back to the kitchen area.

"Yes, troublemaker. Langston told us about how she tried to notify someone of her whereabouts here at the hospital and how he had to put her in a cage just to keep her from screaming the building down. Now she's run off with those three kids, the ones she thinks are 'hers.' What the hell kind of creature is she, anyway?"

Rooney breathed a sigh of relief that it seemed Devan didn't know anything about the stolen wallet. He wasn't sure why he was protecting Belle, but his gut told him she wasn't entirely up to no-good.

"Well, I came to talk to you about something specific."

She sat down at one of the tables and reached

behind her to pull her long, braided hair across her shoulder, fingering the curled ends absently as she waited for him to speak.

"Do you remember how you first found me?"

Blinking, she glanced away and off into space, clearly thinking and trying to remember. "I'm not sure. Seemed like I was playing with my dolls when I heard your voice."

His lips curled into a smile and he pointed his finger at her. "Bingo. My spirit was in your favorite toy. Rollo, the clown."

She gasped and covered her mouth, her eyes sparkling like the little girl she'd been at that time. "Yes! I had just given him a high-five."

Rooney thought about that day. She was so young, but then so was he. He was many human years older than Devan, but in faery years, he was only slightly more aged. They practically grew up together. "Yes, that was the moment. We touched fingers, Devan. That's how we bonded."

"Hmmm…" She considered his words, still not looking at him, caught up in the memory.

"It's time to break that bond, Devvie."

Her eyes widened as she turned to glare at him. "Break it? What does that mean? You've been my friend forever, Roon."

He sat down across from her and reached to place his hand over hers. "We'll always be friends, Devvie. But it's time. You've got Kent now, and I know

Daeglan is hoping for a wedding soon..."

"Father wants it, but Kent hasn't asked."

"Listen, the bond is too intimate for us now. It doesn't do either of us any good that at any time I can close my eyes and see you. I mean, I'm probably lucky I haven't caught a glimpse of your man's junk yet as it is."

"Roon..."

He was skirting around the truth of things, but her pained expression was more than he'd anticipated. Before he'd left Belle in Danville, that simple touching of their hands had bonded him to her. A faery bonded to two people would never work and would probably drive him crazy. He'd heard of it happening. He had to let Devvie go if he was ever going to move on. It was his only chance to make a go of things with Belle. And for whatever reason, the most important thing to him right now was finding out if something could work between him and the lovely siren.

With a deep, forlorn sigh, Devan pulled her hand from under his and used it to cup his cheek. "You're sure?"

He took the chance to kiss her palm. "Yeah, Devvie. I'm sure."

"So how do we do this? If I have to kiss you or something, Kent's not going to like it."

"Pfft!" he scoffed. "Not a kiss. You've got to slap me."

"Slap you! On the face?"

Rooney's eyes twinkled as he stood and grinned. "Nah, you gotta slap me on my arse." And he turned to present her with his backside.

"Sicko."

His face got serious, and he rotated back around to face her. "You remember how you had to let me go when you conjured me from the faery realm that time?" He knew she knew. It was the night they'd kissed. It was the night he had discovered she would never love him the way he loved her—the way he'd thought he did, anyway. She nodded now in answer. "Just say *an deireadh* and let me go."

Part of him expected it to be difficult for her to release him, but she did it in an instant when she repeated the words "the end" in Gaelic. The line between them severed just in the blink of an eye, and he was left without her, the friend he'd touched mentally since they were both merely children. His eyes stung with tears.

When he closed them to find his control, he saw Belle, her face soft in sleep, stretched out on the couch in the cabin. He thought in that moment that he could watch her like that forever. Then, no, he thought he'd like to hold her instead forever.

"Roon?"

His eyes snapped open when Devan spoke, and he forced a smile. "Thanks, Devvie."

She cocked her head to the side and looked at him with narrow eyes. "This has to do with that girl, doesn't it? That's really what's going on, isn't it?"

He couldn't answer because "that girl's" voice intruded in his mind. Belle murmured his name in terror, and without speaking another word to Devan, he conjured the golden door to get back to her.

Chapter FOURTEEN

Belle's body told her she needed a nap, but her mind was whirling with thoughts of the kiss with Roon. At first she told herself that maybe she was just relieved he wouldn't cause trouble for her about stealing the wallet. Then she decided her reaction to him must be gratitude that he was willing to stick around to help her.

The truth was, she wanted that man in a way she'd never wanted anyone before. His very presence in a room was like a magnetic pull on all of her cells at once. She was drawn to him, wanting to touch him and kiss him again.

Plopping down on the couch, she lay back and closed her eyes, trying to calm her speeding heart. When she placed her hand against the pounding in her chest, she thought of Roon's hand instead and imagined him placing his palm in just that very same spot. Her nipples tightened, and all sorts of erotic imaginings coursed through her mind.

She bit her lip and willed her mind away from wantonness, but from her toes to the top of her head she felt flushed with desire. Tightening her legs together, she allowed her lip to slip from between her teeth with a breathy sigh.

"I smell your lust," a gravelly voice said, breaking through her wild imaginings, and she bolted upright in panic, a scream tearing through her lips. The man slapped his hand over her mouth to silence her before speaking close to her ear. "Lodar will like that musky smell on you, assuming that lust is for him."

She could hear her breath rushing in and out of her nose as panic welled up in her. Her eyes glanced at the window, but she couldn't see the children. It was daylight so Lodar couldn't be there—at least not out in the open. No, instead he'd sent his werewolf cronies to find her. She turned her attention to the huge man crouching beside the couch. He released her mouth but anticipated her next move, and his hand clawed her wrist, unwilling to let her bolt away.

She shook her head, swallowing hard as she tugged to get free of him. She heard a cry from outside and the sound ripped through her heart. Tears welled in her eyes when she realized it was one of the children—probably Lena.

Her thoughts turned back to the red-haired faery, only this time not with longing but in pleading. *Rooney, where are you? I need you here.*

"Cat got your tongue now, missy? It always does when you're running away."

She willed the words to come, but they wouldn't. Her throat felt closed off, any ability to speak stuffed away and unable to escape. Her tears spilled over as he hauled her to her feet and dragged her outside.

"Belle, they're going to make us go back. Please, Belle, we can't go back." Lena's face was blotchy, red with emotion, and stained with tears as she fought to pull herself away from the black warlock holding her hands behind her back.

A werewolf had Jeremy and Nona, holding each child by the neck of their shirts, one in each hand. The boy kicked the were's shin, but the creature only howled with laughter. Nona was still as stone, her eyes wide and intense. She seemed to be staring off to Belle's right.

"Okay, okay," the warlock spoke. "Get her over here."

Lena twisted her head around and sank her teeth into the man's arm. He screeched and lifted her high then tossed her to the ground a few feet away from him. Belle was horrified when the girl dropped, limp and unmoving.

Once his hands were free, the warlock motioned his hand in front of him and a golden door opened up beside him. Belle looked again at Lena, prostrate on the ground, and she began to struggle anew.

"Let me goooooo!" she screamed, the force of the air booming from her lungs enough to knock her and her captor back. He didn't relinquish his hold on her, but he shook his head, dazed as her cry continued to draw out of her lips.

"Dammit. Now you've done it," Jeremy and Nona's werewolf howled, letting them go so he could slap his hands over his ears.

And then the werewolf was struck by a bolt of green light, and his body sailed back against a nearby tree. Belle stopped screaming and looked in the direction from which the magic had come.

Rooney.

His green eyes were blazing with fury as he jumped at the warlock, jabbing the man in the jaw with a one-two punch and then using his foot to kick him into the dirt. Belle was so entranced by his heroics that at first she didn't even notice he hadn't come to her rescue alone.

Flashes of magic to her opposite side caught her attention, and she saw Devan, her long brown locks wild and curly all around her body, her hands pressed forward as she used her magic to shove the one werewolf back away from the children.

The were holding Belle let go of her, taking a few steps away so that he could shift into his wolf form. She watched his body contort and squirm and bend into that of a massive beast before he turned his attention to Devan.

The witch didn't show a bit of concern. She just put her hands up over her head and crouched down. When the wolf attempted to pounce on her, he was deflected by an invisible bubble surrounding her.

"Belle, get the children. Take them inside," she instructed, flicking her head towards the cabin as she slapped both werewolves with energy orbs to keep them at bay.

Belle gathered the children like chicks and motioned them to the door, helping the dazed Lena move on wobbly feet. Over her shoulder, she glanced back at Rooney, who was still wrestling with the warlock. One of the werewolves got away from Devan and ran towards her. She used one hand to gently shove the last child inside, then charged back at the were, screaming low in her throat.

Just as he was about to reach her, the wolf suddenly howled, staggered back, and then fell over. He kicked his hind legs a few times before taking a long breath and then going completely still.

"How the hell did you do that?" Devan demanded. Belle looked up at the woman and saw her staring down at the prostrate animal, her eyes wide in wonder. The other werewolf was also lying on the ground, but he had a sharp piece of wood sticking out of his side.

"She's got a bag of tricks even she doesn't know about," Rooney said from behind Devan, dragging the kicking and screaming warlock behind him.

Belle looked back at the werewolf she had struck down. The honest truth was that she had no idea how she had bested him. The fact that she hadn't been alone empowered her in a way she'd never been before, so instinct kicked in. She knelt down in the dirt beside him and saw to her horror that blood was trickling out of both of his ears. "Is he dead?"

"'Fraid so, princess. Fortunately, this guy's not," Rooney groaned as he hauled the warlock to his feet and shoved him against a tree. "How 'bout it, dude. Who the hell sent you here?"

"She knows." He inflected his head to point his chin in Belle's direction. "She knows he won't stop until he has her."

Devan had her hands behind her head, braiding her hair again, but her face was scrunched into a frown. "Who won't?"

A breath Belle didn't realize she'd been holding escaped her lips, and without thinking, she reached a hand up and touched Rooney's shoulder. "It's Lodar. I belong to him."

Chapter
FIFTEEN

"I thought you belonged to the Bittners. That's where Nicky and Gerry found you," Rooney heard Devan say, wary confusion in her voice. He wasn't looking at her though. He was still holding on to the warlock, but his neck was contorted so that he could look into Belle's eyes. He could see the fear churning in her gaze, though she held herself tall and stoic.

"I did. I was one of their children. Legally, I'm their daughter. What I mean by belong is that...Lodar expects me to marry him. In a few months, actually."

"Marriage?" Rooney felt the word claw its way out

of his throat. "You want to marry that damned bloodsucker?"

Lodar wasn't just any vampire. He was the one the Women wanted. The one who had killed Báisteach's son, Craig. Rooney was supposed to help Devan find him, to deliver him back to the faery realm so the Women could exact whatever punishment they deemed. But even though they'd captured him for a short time, he managed to get away from them less than twenty-four hours later.

"Did you agree to marry him?" asked Devan. Roon could feel her eyes boring into him, but he couldn't meet her gaze. Marriage? Belle was seriously supposed to marry that vampire?

"I was just a girl when I said yes. I thought he loved me. He courted me just like out of one of the regency novels I liked to read as a teenager. I thought it was what I wanted, but then I found out the truth."

Rooney could see the tears building in her eyes, tears she was determined not to let fall. "How old were you?"

"Sixteen when I told him I'd marry him. Seventeen by the time we told the Bittners. I knew what the vampires did. I knew the reason they had us there. But I never knew how they did it. I never knew how vicious they could be. When I saw him... Lodar..." She shook her head wild, her black locks falling into her face. "I told him I couldn't do it, that I couldn't marry him. He was furious, said he wouldn't ever let me go. "

"I think you should take them home with you, Roon," Devan told him, tapping him on the elbow to draw his attention. "This place was safe at one time, but I guess probably the entire Org knows about it after our battle here months ago." She glanced out at the forest. "They could have people watching us now."

The warlock started shoving against Rooney's grasp. "Let me go!" he cried, desperation in his eyes. "C'mon, you're not gonna get anything from me so just let me go."

"What makes you think I'm finished with you?" Rooney grinned, though the expression was wicked instead of playful. He kicked the warlock in the shin then turned back to Devan. "You're probably right…"

His words trailed off when he felt the hand holding the man begin to heat up. When he looked, he saw a blazing red glow surrounding the warlock. For a moment, he thought the man was trying to escape his grasp, but the look in his eyes was one of terror. After just a few seconds, the heat was such that Rooney had to pull his hand away. A moment more and the warlock went up in a ball of white flame. He was screaming and crying for mercy.

A sound behind them had everyone pivoting to look, and the two werewolves' bodies were also aflame, burning and sizzling like a science experiment gone bad. When the three of them were nothing but burnt carcasses, all eyes turned to Belle. She was deathly pale, one trembling hand at her throat.

"Is this more of your bag of tricks?" Devan asked, her eyes narrowed.

Belle shook her head. "I didn't do that. I don't know how that happened."

Rooney could see Devvie didn't trust Belle, but he knew without a doubt she was telling the truth. He didn't know everything there was to know about a siren's powers, but he was pretty sure sending a body up in flames wasn't one of them. Besides that, the look in her eyes was enough to tell him she wasn't responsible.

"He wanted to be let go pretty badly," he spoke, turning his eyes to the tree line. "Seemed like he wasn't all that scared of us, as much as he was desperate to get out of here. You think they might have been spelled?"

"For what purpose?" Devan asked.

"To keep them from talking. Maybe they were given a set amount of time to get back with Belle. Seems kind of crazy, but Lodar's a conniving guy."

Silence settled in on them. Rooney dropped his hand to his side and reached out his pinky to touch Belle's arm. She didn't flinch or move away. She just cut her eyes over to him.

"Can we come out?" Lena's voice broke the quiet. She was peeking out of a small crack in the door.

Rooney watched Belle's body relax as she nodded her head. "Yes, come on, children. We all should thank Ms. Devan and Rooney."

A laugh welled up in Roon's chest, but he choked

it down. Sometimes Belle reminded him of a school marm, but he didn't figure she'd appreciate that analogy. "No thanks necessary, but I'm thinking it is about time for us to take a trip. What do you think, Belle?"

"Aw, man!" Jeremy wailed. "We just got here. Not another road trip."

Belle gave the slightest of nods to let Rooney know she was in agreement. He grinned and leaned to put his hand down on the boy's head. "This won't be another road trip, and I guarantee you that you'll like where we're going."

"Okay," Devan spoke. "Everyone should probably get their things together. I'll open the golden door when you're ready."

When the kids bounded back into the house, Belle approached Devan. She stopped just in front of the other woman, then reached into her back pocket to pull out a little notebook. Without a word she handed it to Devan.

"What's this?" Devan frowned in confusion.

"This is a list of the money I owe you," Belle told her, dropping her eyes to the ground for a moment before looking back up to meet Devan's gaze. "I took your wallet. We used your money and credit cards to get here. I don't know what this cabin cost because Rooney said he took care of it."

Rooney came up behind Devan's back and looked over her shoulder, taking stock of the meticulous ledger of expenses written in the notebook. At the top, it read, "Pay Back to Devan."

"I promise, I'll repay you. I'll find some sort of job or something wherever we're going, and I'll give you every penny back. And I apologize. I'm truly sorry, but..." Belle shook her head. "No, no explanations. I'm sorry."

Devan nodded, and Belle wrung her hands a moment before rushing up the steps and into the cabin to help the children gather their things. Rooney's chest swelled with emotion, not the smallest of which was pride. He knew how difficult that must have been for his princess.

"Rooney..."

He glanced back at Devan, a goofy smile on his face.

"Did you know about this?"

He scratched his head and squinted his eyes. "I'd better go help them get their things together."

Chapter
SIXTEEN

The world before Belle was like none she would ever have imagined. She could actually hear the colors. They snapped and popped and crackled in all directions. A sweet scent wafted through the air, something like a fruit, but she couldn't pin down which one. With a deep breath, she dropped both hands limp at her sides and looked up at the sky in awe.

"Quite a place, huh?" Rooney asked, and she could hear the spike of pride in the tone of his voice.

"It is. It's remarkable," she agreed, nodding before looking down at the children. They were standing in a line, tallest to shortest, gazing around at the scenery.

"I felt the same way when I came here the first time," Devan said as she closed the golden door behind her. "It's like a fairy tale." Then she giggled at her own joke.

The place didn't feel like a "fairy tale" to Belle. It felt strangely like home. Like she was finally in the place she was always meant to be. The human world was dull, void, and silent compared to this place. The thought that she would eventually have to go back to her own home made her heart ache.

"Look at that!" Jeremy cried and ran towards a tree with low-hanging limbs. Just as he was about to leap onto those limbs, Belle felt an audible vibration rap from the roots of the tree in her direction.

In reaction, she ran to the boy and grabbed him by the arm, stopping him before he could pounce onto the tree. "She doesn't like to be climbed on."

Jeremy honored the serious character of her voice by stopping and placing his hands behind his back like a child caught with his hand in the cookie jar.

"How do you know that?" Rooney queried, coming around to step in front of her so he could peer into her eyes. "I mean, it's common knowledge around here that the Bructenlilly tree doesn't care for folks climbing on its branches, but how could you know that?"

Belle shrugged, keeping her demeanor passive as she suffered his intense glare. "The tree told me." She could see the gears turning in Rooney's head as he tried to decipher what was happening, but she looked away before he could say anything else.

"This doesn't look like the Summer. I thought we'd be bringing them to your home, Roon," Devan said, stepping lightly in a circle and peering at the sun overhead.

"This is the Fall," Roon nodded, staring at Belle a few more moments before turning his attention back to Devan. "I decided it was best for us to come here, so these are the directions I gave you for opening the door. I guess we probably should've brought everyone a jacket, huh?"

Devan grinned and twirled her hand, conjuring several light coats and handing them out to everyone. Miraculously, each one fit the wearer perfectly.

"C'mon," Rooney urged. "My parents' place is just up over that hill."

Belle almost laughed at Devan's bug-eyed expression. "You have parents?"

"Pfft!" Rooney scoffed then pointed up the hillock so that the kids knew they could run along. "Of course I have parents. What, did you think I just sprouted up out of the ground or something?"

Devan pursed her lips a moment, clearly perturbed with her friend. Belle's eyes intently watched as the lovely brunette shoved at Rooney with one hand while at the same time smiling at him. A pang shot through her as she recognized their banter for what it was. Flirting. She thought back to Rooney's words to her earlier that day. *I'd do anything for Devvie.*

"I thought you were with Kent," Belle heard herself saying before she could stop herself. Her cheeks and Devan's simultaneously reddened, and after a second, Belle couldn't bring herself to stand there looking silly anymore. She hissed air from between her lips and marched off to catch up with the children.

"Hey," Rooney said close to her ear when he caught up with her. "Devvie is with Kent. We're just fooling around."

She side-eyed daggers at him and kept walking, trying to get away from him.

She squealed like one of the children when she felt Rooney's hand at her rear, pinching her. "What the hell do you think you're doing?"

He slipped in behind her, leaning back against a tree and snaking his hand around her waist to pull her against him, her backside to his front. She could feel his hard body pressed against her, and the muscles between her legs tightened in reaction.

"Princess," he whispered against her neck, rustling her black locks with his warm breath. "It may be true that I wanted more from Devvie than friendship at one time, but there is only one woman who has ever lit a fire under me like the one that's burning me up right now." His hand slipped low to rest against her abdomen, tugging her rear end snug against his hot, hard erection. "I want *you*, Belle. I want to drop you on that grass, take off every bit of clothing separating us, and then I want to—"

"Belle!" Lena's voice interrupted him, and when the girl's dark head popped up from the top of the hill, Belle slapped at Rooney's hands and took a huge step away from him. She heard him chuckling behind her, but instead of looking at him, she trudged up to where the children were calling her name.

Chapter
SEVENTEEN

It occurred to Rooney that Belle was likely to be the death of him. He reached down to tug at the crotch of his jeans as he walked the long way around the hill just before his parents' home. He needed a few moments to settle himself down before going into anyone else's presence. A glance over his shoulder told him that Devan was following Belle and the kids instead of him. He breathed a sigh of relief.

The hill over which the rest of his party climbed wasn't very wide, and he only had to walk about one hundred yards out of the way to get around it. He came upon the same spot they were in just a few moments after them. By that time, his mom was exiting the cottage, wiping her hands on her apron with a puzzled yet pleasant look on her face.

"'Lo, Mom!" he called out to her, waving his hands to draw her attention. She brushed a few curly locks from her brow before cupping her hand above her eyes to block the sun.

"Albert? Is that you, son? You know I can't see a thing, so come closer, boy."

He chuckled and rolled his eyes before sprinting forward to take her into a huge hug, picking her portly figure off her feet and twirling her. "Of course, it's me, Mom. I'm the only one of your children who would pop in without letting you know I was coming."

She chortled and slapped at his shoulders until he let her go. Then to cool her own excitement she patted her pink cheeks a few times with the backs of her. "And who have you here with you? Friends?"

She said the word friends with a certain tone even as her eyes flicked from Devan to Belle and back again a few times. He knew just what she was thinking. She had a gaggle of grandchildren from her daughters, yet she still always fretted about him bringing home a "pretty girl."

It suddenly occurred to Rooney how strange life could be. He had never once brought a woman home to meet his parents, and he'd often dreamed of the day that he would finally bring Devan here. How ironic that here he was, Devvie in tow, but the one he truly wanted his mother to know was Belle.

"Mom, this is Devan." He motioned his BFF forward, and she grinned as she extended her hand.

"Devvie? Finally you've brought your dear friend Devvie to meet us. He's told us much about you."

Devan laughed and glanced at him through the corner of her eye. "And he's said so much about you too…" She hesitated, and he knew she wasn't sure what to call the woman. They didn't really have surnames in the faery realm. His mother saved him.

"Oh, please just call me DeeDee. No one really calls me Dierdre."

"And these little ones are Lena, Jeremy, and Nona." Rooney pointed to the children one by one as he introduced them.

The children were polite and inclined their heads in acknowledgment, sweet smiles on their faces. Belle was standing just behind them, her hands behind her back, eyes unblinking as she waited.

Rooney decided to make a statement. He stepped up beside her and placed his hand gently at Belle's back. He felt a tremble course through her, and it was all he could do not to grin over the fact that his touch could illicit such a reaction. "Mom," he said. "This is Belle."

Even if his mother didn't catch on to the special tone in his voice when he said her name and urged her forward, he knew that Belle had detected the distinct importance he was putting on their introduction. Still, she kept her straight-backed composure and stepped forward like royalty with hand extended. "DeeDee, it is a pleasure."

"Oh, my. You are truly a Belle, aren't you, lass?"

That broke Belle's composure for the briefest of seconds, her eyes blinking once and then twice.

"It is a good thing I managed some extra game this evening." A rumbling voice spoke behind them, and Rooney turned to smile at his father. "It seems we'll have a full table."

"Hey, Pop," he said, stepping forward to clasp hands, wrapping one arm around his sire's burly shoulders in a manly embrace. "It's good to see you."

"If it were so good, you'd come home more often."

Rooney made another round of introductions, presenting his father by his given name of Albert.

"She called *you* Albert, didn't she?" Lena asked, a frown crinkling her forehead.

"Ah, well, I don't really go by that name, but moms are allowed to call their children anything they want, I suppose."

Everyone laughed even as DeeDee blushed a bit, again cooling her cheeks with her hands.

"I'll actually need to be going," Devvie announced after a moment. "We left so fast I didn't really tell Kent what was going on, and he'll be climbing the walls soon."

"Are you sure you can't stay for dinner?" DeeDee

asked, her eyes expectant.

Rooney saw the discomfort in Devvie's eyes. She hated disappointing anyone. He stepped forward to save her, placing a hand on her shoulder. "She's got lots going on, Mom, and her boyfriend will be worried."

DeeDee nodded in understanding. Then they all watched as Devan opened the golden door and stepped into it. After just a moment, the door closed up, and she was gone.

"Well," DeeDee sighed. "We should get ready for a big meal then. Would you girls come inside and help me prepare? I think it will take all hands to cut up the vegetables."

The ladies all went inside, and Rooney could see Jeremy standing there, a bit dumbfounded. He glanced up at his father and saw the elder man's thoughtful expression.

"Do you know how to fish, Jeremy? I've got a pole we can take down to the river. You can practice while Rooney and I dress the meat for dinner."

The boy's eyes lit up with enthusiasm, and they all headed off to the water's edge.

Albert was a patient man, not only in his instructions to Jeremy about fishing but also in the way that he silently waited for his son to speak. Rooney and his father were a close pair, and even in his wildest days, Roon had never failed to 'fess up to Albert about his actions or seek his counsel when he needed it.

And he needed it now. The weight of the last few

days settled over him like an anvil the moment he crossed back over into the faery realm. The pull of the Women was palpable, like an invisible line connected to his gut that urged him back to the gray hill. The Women always knew when someone crossed over. They would want a report about the search for Lodar, Craig's killer.

"What do you think of Belle?" Roon asked as he worked at skinning one of the rabbits his father had killed.

"She's a lovely girl. I always expected you to bring Devan to meet us, but I was a bit surprised to make the acquaintance of the other."

"Yes, I was surprised too, Pop."

"Your mother's going to enjoy having the children around. She misses your nieces and nephews. You do plan on having them stay with us?"

He nodded. "My place isn't anywhere big enough for all of us."

"You'll be staying too, then?"

There was an amused glint in Albert's eyes even though he didn't take his gaze from his work.

Rooney imagined his parents had waited a long time for him to take serious interest in a woman. They always knew he cared for Devvie, but somehow even they'd sensed it would never come to fruition. The grin on his face fell away, and he fisted his hands for a moment to relieve the building tension in his arms before he spoke. "I've done something. I've done something I'm not sure the Women will appreciate."

Albert stopped his work and turned to face his son. He placed his knife on a stump beside him and leaned one hand against a tree trunk, giving Rooney his undivided attention. "What's happened?"

"I broke the bond with Devvie. I broke it so that I could bond with Belle."

Albert took a long breath and slowly moved his head up and down. "It was to be expected. Devan never to belonged to you. The Women must know this."

"I don't know, Pop. I have a bad feeling. The bond with Devvie let me keep track of her, of what she was doing in going after the Org."

"And of course in her ability to open and close the door between the realms."

Rooney pursed his lips and frowned. Yes, there was that. For all of these years, the human and faery realms were separated so that no magical creature could cross over from one to the other without losing their powers. Devan's magic had changed that. She bridged the worlds to make it possible for any creature to pass from one realm to the other. And it was only natural that the Women would be concerned about that and the protection of the faery realm.

"That isn't all." He raised his eyes to look at his father. "Belle is a siren."

Albert's startled expression sent prickles of alarm across Rooney's arms. His father looked more than just a little concerned—he was well and truly worried. "Are you certain?"

"Pretty certain. You should see the things she can do." And he related the actions he'd witnessed from Belle since that first day he found her humming to block the sound of fighting with the Org. "I didn't think they existed."

Albert's frown put deep creases into his forehead. He rubbed at the back of his neck and glared at the ground. "They don't anymore. At least they aren't supposed to. And the Women will surely know she's here."

"What should I do?"

After slapping Rooney reassuringly on the back, Albert returned to the chore of dressing his rabbit. "Let me give it some thought, son."

Chapter
EIGHTEEN

Belle opened her eyes from one of the deepest sleeps she could remember ever having. She flicked her gaze back and forth in the darkness, the only light in the room coming from a moon outside the window. Disoriented, she tried to remember where she was.

The feeling of vibrations from all around reminded her of the sensations she'd felt the moment she'd entered the faery realm. She knew she was at Rooney's parents' house, but she couldn't remember how she got into this room. Or the cozy bed upon which she was snuggled.

The last thing she recalled was DeeDee insisting she sit because she'd looked "completely and utterly exhausted." DeeDee had been right. The drive plus the fight with Lodar's werewolves had sapped almost every last ounce of energy she'd had.

You okay, princess?

She gasped and sat up, clutching the blanket to her chin. She wasn't sure why she did that as she was still fully clothed.

"Rooney? Are you in here?" she whispered.

In your mind, princess. I'm talking to you telepathically. Think it, don't say it.

A frown scrunched her brow up tight as she tried to figure out what he was telling her to do. She'd never communicated with anyone telepathically, and she was sure she couldn't possibly do so now.

Like...this? she finally managed, feeling a little silly.

Ha! I knew you'd get it pretty quickly. How are you feeling? You barely even moved when I carried you to my room.

Belle blinked a few times then threw back the covers and dropped her feet over the side of the bed. *I'm fine. If I'm in your room, where are you?*

I'm in the living room, in Pop's chair. The children are in the room that used to be my sisters' room. You hungry?

Her stomach growled, and she placed a palm to her abdomen, nodding to herself. *I could eat.*

C'mon into the kitchen. I'll meet you there.

She managed to figure out that she needed to turn left once outside of the bedroom. When she got into the kitchen, she saw Rooney slicing a block of cheese and placing the pieces onto a plate with some crusty bread.

"I thought you'd want to eat when you woke up," he whispered, glancing over his shoulder at her. "I couldn't keep a bowl of Mom's stew warm so I made sure we saved some bread for you. Those kids of yours are porkers. They each ate at least two bowls."

Belle snatched a slice of bread from the plate and nibbled it while he spoke.

"I can't really blame the kids though. Nothing like Mom's cooking. I usually just stick with vegetables and breads at my place."

"Where is your place?"

He smiled at her and popped a slice of cheese into his mouth. After swallowing, he spoke again. "I live in the Summer. I take after my mom, and that's the climate she prefers. But the Fall is Pop's home so…"

"So she just gave up her home to live here?"

His grin turned lopsided, giving his eyes a cocky glint. "Yeah, that seems to be the thing to do when you're in love."

She felt him watching her for a reaction, but she couldn't think of anything to say. Instead, she just continued munching on the bread and cheese.

"Let's go outside so we don't wake anyone up."

Moving her head up and down in agreement, she

watched him grab a few blankets from the chair in the living area and then followed him outside.

The evening sky was breathtaking, a dark purple with stars that twinkled in every color of the rainbow. Belle stood there with her mouth agape, appreciating the gorgeous sight and even catching the flash of a shooting star just above the golden moon.

"The place is utterly magical," she breathed.

Rooney's hand settled at the small of her back, urging her toward a tree. He draped one of the blankets onto the grass before dropping down to sit and lean his back against the trunk. She watched the tree carefully, reading its vibrations for objection but detecting none. When her eyes flicked back to him, she saw one of his arms reaching for her.

Not giving herself time to think about it, she took his offered hand and let him pull her down to sit between his legs. She wiggled to and fro a moment, finding just the right spot before releasing a deep breath. She thought she felt a rumble in his chest, like he was chuckling at her. Then he took the other blanket and wrapped it around the both of them.

Her long black hair fell across one shoulder, and Rooney began to comb his fingers through the locks, the slow, easy ministrations relaxing her almost to sleep. "I like that," she admitted, laying her head back against his chest.

"You surprise me, you know. Almost everything in your gestures screams, 'Stay back, don't touch,' and yet you seem to give in to my attention so easily."

Belle grinned and slid her head back and to the side so she could look at up him. "You almost sound disappointed by that. Do you prefer the chase?"

"Ha! Not really. I feel like I've been chasing things all my life. It's kinda nice to think my charm is winning for once."

She pondered this a few moments, twisting her lip to the side as she considered him. "You mean Devan? You really cared for her, didn't you? Your mom mentioned she thought you'd bring her home one day."

He groaned and hid his eyes with his palm, rubbing his forehead. "Moms."

"Well, she did say she was really happy to have us here. She fawned over the children like they were her own grandchildren. I think she's lonely, Rooney."

The fingers brushing her hair stopped, clenching the locks a moment before splaying again. "Yes, she is. My youngest sister married just a few months ago. Her last chick has left the nest, and all of them live in other seasons."

The silence between them should have been uncomfortable, but Belle had never felt more at ease before in her life. The air hummed smooth, wafting with the scent of wet grass. She rolled around, curling herself up so that she could lay her cheek on his chest. His heart thumped in a rhythm that matched her own. Somehow, she felt like they were one.

"I've never done that telepathy thing before. I

thought I knew most of my powers, but that was one I wasn't aware of having."

"Belle." He brought his hand around so that his thumb could caress her cheek. "There's something I need to tell you about that."

A little flame developed in her chest, and she licked her lips, trying to concentrate on his words but wanting more than anything to kiss him.

"That telepathy thing wasn't a power, necessarily. That was a bond. You and I, we're bonded."

She flattened both palms on his chest and held herself away from him so she could study his eyes. "What does that mean exactly? And how did we get bonded? We haven't even...you know." She could only hope he couldn't see her blush in the moonlight.

"It happened back at the cabin when we touched hands. I couldn't have forced you to bond with me, Belle. Your heart had to be open to me, and it was."

A pain was developing in the center of her forehead. Her third eye again. She closed her eyes and tried to imagine the tension easing away. "I wish that didn't mean I was so transparent to you."

"Princess, that's what love is. It opens you wide, reveals your soul, makes you vulnerable, but it also makes you available to get so much more."

"The bond is how you knew I was in trouble, isn't it?"

He nodded. "I heard you calling for me in your mind. All you ever have to do is call for me, and I'll come for you."

She thought about all of the times she might have needed someone, anyone in the past. In truth, she'd had it easier than some supplicant children. And as she got older, she could have been traded off. Instead, the Bittners had found a place for her in their household. They'd acquired the other children who immediately became like true family to her, but still she'd been alone. In the sense of adulthood, it was just Belle. She had to take care of herself. She had to take care of her children.

"You can tell me, you know. You can tell me anything about those days if you want."

She'd been holding her body up, but when he said those words, her muscles quivered and she fell against him. She refused to cry, so instead she just clutched at his shirt with balled fists and held her face hard into his chest.

"I first met Devvie when she was just a very little girl. Her father barely paid her any attention. She was so lonely, so tiny and afraid. I was a kid, too, and when the Women told me to bond with her, it was easy. I wanted to be her best friend..."

Somehow he understood that she needed to get her emotions under control. Instead of pressing her to talk, he chose to do the talking for her. He started with the early days, how his friendship progressed with Devan, how she was sent to therapy and forced to block him out, how he finally connected with her again when she discovered her powers.

"The Women take care of this world. They watch over us, provide for the natural order of things here. And now the Women have another assignment for me—for Devan and me. They want us to deliver Lodar to them."

She twitched in his arms, keeping her head down and not looking at him. "Lodar? What do they want with him? He's just another member of the Org."

Rooney caressed her hair, tightened one arm around her, and kissed her forehead. "He's not just another member. Báisteach is the central Woman, the giver of water and rain and life. Lodar killed her son, and she wants him to answer for it."

"But how did he kill her son? I thought the doors to cross over were closed?"

"Her son chose not to cross over during the Time of Choosing. A *seelie faery* remains as a perpetual child, and he became one of Lodar's supplicants."

She sat up then and looked at him, her mind spinning with thoughts.

Chapter
NINETEEN

Rooney stared hard into Belle's eyes, trying to decipher the haunted look behind her gaze. He placed a feather soft caress on her arm, and she shivered before leaning her back against him again.

"He said there was one special child, one that he lost. He regretted that."

Snorting with disdain, Rooney shook his head. "Regretted? Belle, what exactly went on with you and Lodar?"

He didn't want to think about the relationship between Lodar and Belle, but he couldn't stop himself from asking. It was a double-edged sword; the truth might destroy any chance they would have of being together, but he still had to know.

"I was just a teenager," she began, settling back against him and wrapping her arms around his waist. "The Bittners were always entertaining. They loved the social opportunities of their position with the Org and played it up. But that meant there were always a lot of eyes on me. Men's eyes. Maybe I looked like an easy target."

More likely her looks were impossible to deny. Belle was absolutely breathtaking, and he imagined that even in her youth, she had them drooling for her. Couple that with her siren's powers, which must have been burgeoning at that time, and it certainly would have made her almost irresistible.

"So I wasn't unused to the attention, but the Bittners kept most of them at bay. They expected strict decorum in their household, as ironic as that seems, all things considered. Whatever they did to me as a child, they weren't unkind to me—just austere. So anyway, Lodar was different than the other men. I liked him. I'll never forget how he took my hand and kissed it the first time he was introduced to me."

A red-hot poker jabbed into Rooney's stomach as he imagined the scene. The breathy tone of Belle's voice was clear enough. She was recalling a fond memory, and that meant she must have cared for the vampire.

"You loved him," he murmured. It was more of a statement than a question.

Her head rubbed against his chest, shaking back and forth. "No, I didn't love him. I liked him. I guess, thinking back on it now, I must have liked the idea of him. What is it they say about some people? Maybe I was just in love with being in love. I liked his attention. I liked the way he courted me. He treated me like I was royalty. Like a princess." She hesitated, and he knew she was thinking of the way he used that same endearment for her. "And when I was seventeen, he told the Bittners he wanted to marry me."

"And you said yes."

She shrugged her shoulders. "Of course. Why wouldn't I? I had no direction otherwise. I was an adopted child of the Bittners. What was I going to grow up to be? To do? Marrying a high level Org vampire was...appropriate."

"So why didn't you marry him?"

A long breath rushed from her lips. Then another. She swallowed before speaking again. "I specifically requested Nona. The Bittners were looking for another child, but they chose her because I'd asked for her."

It seemed like she was going off on a tangent. He wanted to press her to get on with it, but he was afraid she'd tense up and refuse to finish the story. And he had to know the ending. He had to know there *was* an ending for Belle and Lodar.

"I found him with her. She was so little, too little to

be fed upon. The Bittners always used the reverie, hypnotizing us so that we wouldn't know what was happening during the act. I'd never watched a vampire feeding. It was the most horrific thing I'd ever seen. And she was awake, Roon. That poor little girl was awake the entire time."

"Nona..." He murmured the girl's name, thinking of her sweet angelic face. His gut clenched into a tight ball, but he refrained from doing what would have been natural for him in that moment—namely punching the tree behind them and then kicking it for good measure, all while imagining it was Lodar.

"So you saved her?"

"Yes, but it wasn't just that. I finally came to realize what my life would be like as his wife. I would be his magical connection, the one to screen his supplicants, to bring child after child to him for that dirty business. I abhorred that I had even considered it. That was when I made the plan to get away. I knew I would keep Lena and Jeremy and Nona safe until I could get them the hell out of that place."

"You're safe here, Belle. With me, you're safe."

She didn't answer, and she didn't move. Her body suddenly felt cold against him and still as stone. Rooney placed his hands on her shoulders and slid them down her arms, splaying his fingers when he reached her hands so he could entwine them with hers. She clenched her hand tight with his.

Rooney used his magic to switch positions, orbing

from the spot behind her to just in front of her. The move was so fast that her body didn't even have time to fall backwards without his to prop it up. He embraced her in his arms, easing her back onto the blanket, her black hair fanning out behind her in a dark halo.

Both hands cupped her face as he leaned down to kiss her. Her eyes widened as she watched him descend so close that their breaths mingled. Rooney stopped short, studying her gaze and seeking her soul inside those eyes.

"Say something," he told her.

She swallowed and licked her lips. "What do you want me to say?"

He grinned. "You could have said anything, princess. I just wanted to be sure you weren't frozen the way you do when you get scared."

She shook her head. "I'm not scared of you, Rooney. I'm anything but scared of you."

He kissed her then, gently, but she moaned and her hips arched up. That was when his thin thread of control snapped. He pressed himself against her, grinding her pelvis until she spread her legs to him. They were still fully clothed and he wanted to rectify that immediately, but his sex-clouded mind paused long enough to wonder if he should really try to make love to her here in the middle of the woods outside his parents' house.

"Rooney, don't stop kissing me. I need to feel you kissing me. It's the only thing that makes me forget all of those other things."

Hell yes, he thought to himself. *I damn sure do want to make love to her here.*

Chapter
TWENTY

Belle felt heat creep up from the pit of her stomach and head straight into her cheeks when she heard Rooney's thoughts. *I damn sure do want to make love to her here.* She was part embarrassed, part shocked. Embarrassed because honestly she was so naïve she hadn't realized where their actions were heading; shocked because...well, because making love was exactly where their actions were heading.

No matter all the men who had wanted to, no matter Lodar who pledged his love, promised to marry her—Belle Bittner was still a virgin.

For the moment, she set her worries aside because Rooney definitely seemed to know what he was doing. He kissed her again, his lips slanting over hers and his tongue making movements that had that heat welling up inside of her again.

But this heat headed a different direction—directly to a spot between her legs. Belle moaned and reached her hands down to his backside to bring him harder against her. She ached for him in a way she'd never experienced before.

"Easy, princess. I'm not in any hurry."

She was in a hurry. She was desperate to explore these sensations, and instinctively she knew they would only get better and better. Roon's lips seared a line from her mouth down her neck. He nipped at the sensitive skin at the base of her throat then licked a path lower. His hands were at the hem of her shirt, pulling it up and over the mounds of her breasts. She could feel her nipples tightening in anticipation of his touch, but he didn't dally there for now. Instead he finished removing her shirt and leaned back on his elbows to gaze at her.

"I've wanted this for what seems like a long time, princess. Not really so long because it's only been days."

"What? What have you anticipated?" Her words gushed out in a breathy whisper.

"This." He leaned down and circled the tip of her breast with his lips, wetting the cup of her silky bra and teasing the nipple.

"Oh!" Belle cried, arching her back to him.

The idea of lovemaking always seemed so simple to her. Remove clothing, kiss, have sex. The end. The erotic sensation of him suckling her breast through the fabric of her bra never would have occurred to her. She felt exquisitely naughty.

What Roon was doing to her now was true lovemaking.

He switched to the other breast even as his hands reached behind her to unclip her underclothing. It wasn't hard to do considering her back was still arched to bring him closer and closer to his mouth. After he slipped the bra off, he took a moment to blow his warm, moist breath onto each nipple, and to her surprise and his delight, both of them tightened into even sharper peaks.

"You have the most gorgeous set of breasts, Belle. Truly, absolutely gorgeous." He palmed them for good measure before he slid both hands along the curves on either side of her belly. The sensation was something between ticklish and sensual, but she neither laughed nor made any other sound. It suddenly occurred to her that he was doing all of the work and she was reaping all of the reward. Should she be doing something to him?

"Can I touch you, too?"

His answer sounded more like a groan than an affirmative indication, but she pressed on and delved her hands under his loose shirt. His abdomen was sculpted and harder than she'd expected. He was all jokes and play, and it was strange to imagine that he spent any time working out, but clearly she was wrong.

"You're so…built," she murmured.

"Well, princess, I am the Summer champion of the Games so I'm sort of required to keep myself in shape. Pretty sexy, huh?"

Belle laughed and rolled her eyes. "But you're apparently not required to be humble."

"Hey, let's not discuss my humility right now. Right now, I'd like to see more of you." And with that, he began to work the button of her pants. Belle's breath stuck in her throat as he slid them down her legs, pausing to kiss her hip bones atop the lacy hem of panties. He had her naked of all clothing in the blink of an eye.

It might have been nighttime, but the full moon in the faery realm was amazingly bright. Belle felt starkly exposed as Rooney's green eyes moved slowly up and down the length of her body. The glint in those eyes was intense and hot, and she felt that very same heat pool between her legs.

She found herself quaking in anticipation of what he might do next.

"Sorry, princess. I didn't think about how cold it was out here." He misinterpreted her shiver and reached on either side of him to pull the blanket up tighter around them. The air was a little chilly so she didn't mind the blanket except that now she could feel that Rooney was removing his clothing and she was being denied a chance to look at him.

It didn't take long for that thought to escape her when he settled himself beside her and gently reached his hand to the mound between her legs. She clamped her knees tight in alarm but immediately dropped them apart when she realized she wanted nothing more than to have him touch her there.

He cupped her first, the pressure of his big hand feeling so good she wanted to put her hands on top of his to hold him there tighter. But then he moved his middle finger between her folds to explore more of her.

"Ah, Belle, you're really wet for me, aren't you?"

He slipped one of his fingers inside as his mouth touched her lips again. She sighed into his mouth then raked her fingers through his red hair to hold the kiss. When he pressed a second finger into her slick opening, she thought it couldn't possibly get any better than that. Then he used his thumb to flick her most sensitive spot.

Belle wrenched her mouth from his and cried out, bucking her hips before she could stop herself.

"Easy," he whispered, trailing his lips down her neck. "Easy."

He began a rhythm with her body, strumming her to a fever pitch. Her arms and legs tingled with excitement and all her muscles tightened in anticipation of something she didn't even understand. Her head tilted up and her eyes rolled back in her head in ecstasy.

"Don't stop!" she exclaimed, when he removed his hand.

He chuckled in a deep, throaty manner. "I'm not stopping, Princess." Shifting his body, he moved between her legs. Taking one of her hands in his, he placed her fingers around his member. "It's way too late to stop," he said through gritted teeth.

Her throat constricted as she tightened the hand holding his hot, hard erection.

"Damn, woman," Rooney rasped. "I can't handle too much of that." And he forced her fingers away as he settled himself at her entrance.

"Roon!" She placed a hand on his chest. He gazed down at her, a mixture of what she could only recognize as raw lust but also deep affection in his eyes. "Rooney, you know I care for you, right?"

"Princess, I've known you only a short time, but I damn sure realize we wouldn't be here in our birthday suits about to make love if you didn't feel something for me."

"Okay," she said, her voice small.

He kissed her to cut off any more discussion, and when he did, he also started pressing himself inside her. She was tight and his entrance stretched her in a strange combination of discomfort and pleasure. He kept moving forward, filling her, opening her, connecting his body to hers. He never broke contact with her lips, but he reached a hand down to touch her again, and when he did, her hips thrust forward instinctively.

Something tore inside her when he was forced fully within and she cried out. But the pain lasted only a moment before his soothing ministrations had her humming again with desire and passion.

Then he started moving in and out of her slowly, the friction of his movements exquisite torture. A pulsation started slowly from somewhere deep in her soul. The vibrations in her body worked to meet the ones she sensed in him. They played and strummed in tandem with each other until she felt them align, and in that moment, all consciousness fractured and she screamed his name.

Rooney swallowed the sound, kissing her deep and breathing through her as he too exploded within her.

Chapter
TWENTY-ONE

The world shattered all around Rooney, rippling in on him so that all he could do was cling to Belle. He'd never experienced a release quite like this. When his muscles finally eased, he slid his body to the spot beside her and placed several loving kisses to the tops of her breasts.

He was pleased to see her chest rising and falling with fast breaths, so he knew he wasn't the only one whose world had been rocked—literally. When he looked around, he saw that an assortment of nuts and leaves had dropped from the tree against which they'd made love and he could only marvel that their experience was so strong as to knock them loose from the branches.

"You okay, princess?" he asked her when she didn't move after a few moments.

A beautiful grin spread across her lips, though she kept her eyes closed. "Oh, yes, I'm fabulous."

He chuckled, resting his head in his hand and propping it up on his elbow. He'd realized too late that she was a virgin. He might have been able to muster the effort to stop then, but Belle never gave a single indication that she wanted him to.

She rolled over now and nestled her head into his chest, cuddling close to him. "This is different, Rooney. This really does feel like love."

Reaching down, he tipped her chin so she could look at him. He knew what she meant. She wanted him to know that this wasn't the way she'd felt about Lodar. She wanted him to know that her feelings for him were deeper. "Yes, it is different. It does feel like real love."

And he meant that. He had believed he was in love with Devvie for so long that it didn't occur to him that he might have been just confusing the emotion. The palpitations in his chest when he looked at Belle were wholly different. The way her kisses turned him inside out was nothing like the single kiss he and Devvie had shared.

He loved Belle.

"Did I do all right?" she murmured, ducking her

head a little to hide the blush creeping into her cheeks. He didn't have to see it to know it was there.

"You were perfect. A real sex goddess."

She slapped his chest but giggled. "Rooney..."

"You, princess, put the wow in boomchickawowow."

Her giggle turned to full-out laughter, a deep belly laugh he'd never heard from her before. When she snorted and slapped her hand over her mouth in embarrassment, he too began to laugh. Their guffaws mingled in the cool night air.

"Did you hear that?" Rooney asked suddenly, leaning up and glancing off into the distance.

"I'm pretty sure everyone heard that. We're laughing like a bunch of crazy people."

A deep rumble sounded off in the distance, and Rooney bolted straight up to a sitting position. "Not the laughter. Thunder. And look." He pointed to the sky where clouds were boiling and a bolt of lightning divided the night.

"It's just a storm. We probably should get inside though," Belle said.

He glanced at her and saw that she was slipping back into her clothing. How could she understand the significance of what was going on? Rooney followed her lead though and dressed quickly. They were just picking up the blankets when a little weasel ran up to them, scampering up the blanket so he could perch on Roon's shoulder.

"Robbie?" Rooney asked the critter. "What the hell are you doing here in the Fall?"

"Hey, man, keep it down," the animal hissed. "I came a long way to have a word with you, and it won't do any good for us to get caught."

"Did that thing just talk?" Belle gasped, leaning close to Robbie with wide eyes.

"Shhhh! Geez, didn't you just hear me say to keep it down? We don't have a lot of time."

Belle lowered her voice to a whisper. "Time for what?"

"Listen, man, you know this storm isn't normal. Things are about to get crazy here if you don't report to the Women. Haven't you felt them calling you?"

Rooney swallowed and narrowed his eyes. It was true he had felt the tug in his stomach getting stronger, even to the point of becoming painful. He wasn't ready to face them just yet, but he supposed some things couldn't wait.

"Listen, McKenna sent me to warn you. They know you're here and they know you brought *her*." Robbie nodded his head in Belle's direction. "Báisteach is not happy with you, man."

"Because of Belle? Why would they care about her? I thought this was all about Lodar. And what do you mean McKenna sent you to warn me?"

Robbie the weasel tucked his muzzle close to Rooney's ear. "Don't you know what McKenna's job is? McKenna's entire purpose in life is to spy on the faery realm. She answers to them the same way you do. Except now you aren't keeping them happy and they aren't going to like it."

Taking a deep breath, Roon nodded. "All right. I'll get going. I shouldn't have waited so long to talk to them."

"Wait. McKenna says you should go to the Island Anethemusa first. She says there's someone there you need to speak to."

He was taken aback by the weasel's words. The Island Anethemusa was the place where banished faeries were sent to live out their lives. Stripped of their powers, they were forced to live a difficult existence sans the help of the Women. That meant nature wasn't regulated there, and the land was subject to drought, floods, ice storms, and other natural disasters.

"She says to ask for Aoibhneas. Now I gotta go. Be careful, because someone's always watching."

The critter leaped off Rooney's shoulder and scampered off into the forest. Roon felt Belle place a hand on his shoulder, and he knew she was worried about what was going on.

"Is there trouble, son?"

It was his father's voice, and they both turned to find his parents standing in the cold, glancing nervously at the storms brewing in the sky.

"Yeah, Pop, there's trouble. I need you to take care of Belle and the kids while I go—"

"No!" Belle objected, clutching his arm as if she

would not let him go. "You aren't going by yourself. Whatever's going on has something to do with me, and besides that, I'm not letting you face these Women alone."

DeeDee looked stricken by Belle's words, but Albert smiled in an approving way and nodded. "As it should be. We'll take care of the little ones. You go see to the Women."

"We will, but first..." Rooney stepped closer to his parents so he could lower his voice. "First we're going to the Island Anethemusa. What am I going to find there, Pop?"

Albert took a deep breath as if relieved and at the same time disturbed. "You'll find the truth there, I imagine, son. And before you assume, it's a truth even your mother and I don't know."

Rooney was glad to hear that. His relationship with his parents was strong. He didn't want to imagine there was something they had kept from him.

"There are always rumors," DeeDee spoke. "But it's impossible to know what's true and what's not. Please be careful. The Women won't like you going there." Then she stepped in front of him and stood up on her tiptoes to reach his head and bring it down for her to kiss his cheek.

Belle touched his shoulder to get his attention. "Rooney, I'm going to see the children before we go." It was said in a statement, the way she normally would exclaim her intentions with no expectations she'd get any disagreement. Only he heard the little question in her tone. He looked at her and smiled.

They found the little ones in his sisters' old room. Jeremy was in one bed, his bop dangling from one hand over the side. Belle approached him and caressed his head affectionately before turning to the other direction.

Lena and Nona were together in the other bed. The older girl had all of her limbs strewn out in contorted directions, the way children are so often wont to sleep. Nona looked different. Her entire body was in a little ball, her legs to her stomach and her arms folded under them and against her chest. Her face held a grimace, and he saw her eyes twitching under the lids.

Touching Lena's head in much the same way she had Jeremy's, Belle then leaned over and placed a tender kiss to Nona's cheek. She lingered there a moment, and he could feel the outpouring of love and affection.

"She's dreaming," Belle murmured, her voice cracking just a bit. "She dreams a lot. Wakes with nightmares. It's the only time she shows any sign that she remembers it. What Lodar did, I mean."

His stomach lurched and he swallowed, refusing to let himself get physically ill. With Belle's back still to him, he held out his hand and thought about his wish. When he did, the skin of his palm turned transparent and he saw his veins pulse a fluorescent green.

The first wish was usually frittered away during a faery's youth. Rooney had held his tight, and something in him always expected he'd use it for Devvie. In truth, during his drunken nights in the human world, he'd wondered if there was some way to use it to separate her and Kent. Somehow his conscience had managed to talk him out of it.

So he still had his wish. He watched Belle straighten her back, repossessing her strength and composure. She was strong, and in that moment, he felt certain that no matter what happened with the two of them, they would find a way to get through. They were in charge of their own lives now.

Nona's life was barely starting. She deserved better than to have her youth squandered on nightmares and horrors at the hands of a vampire. As Belle turned back to him, Rooney closed his glowing fist and approached the sweet little girl. He pressed his hand against her head and made his wish.

There would be no more nightmares about Lodar for Belle's little girl.

Chapter
TWENTY-TWO

According to Rooney, it wouldn't be difficult to locate the Island Anethemusa. There was a huge sea that parted the eastern portions of the Fall and the Winter locations in the faery realm. The island was a few miles off the coast and ran almost the entire length of the sea so at any point they could cross the water to get to it.

"But how do we actually get across?" Belle asked, hugging the coat DeeDee had loaned her tight around her body. Even though it was daylight, it still seemed to be getting a lot colder, which according to Rooney didn't make much sense. They were in the Fall, and yet the temps were dropping like it was Winter.

"Swimming would be the easiest, but it's getting a little cold for that. I'm hoping someone will have a boat we can borrow." He switched to sharing thoughts telepathically, and she knew he was worried about other faeries spying on them. *I could open a golden door, but I think that would draw the Women's attention.*

Belle nodded, relieved swimming was out of the question. She didn't want to have to admit to Rooney that she couldn't swim. In fact, she was pretty terrified of water so even the idea of boating across to the island wasn't all that favorable in her mind.

They were walking, holding hands, though Rooney's gait was longer and he was setting a pretty rapid pace. She had to struggle to keep up with him. *Did you know the Women were doing this?*

He glanced at her, frowning. *No, I didn't. I mean, they chose me to work for them, to bond with Devvie, and to be their connection to her in the human world. I always revered the Women, and even over the last several months when I started to resent their meddling, it never once occurred to me that they might spying on all of us. I thought they always had the faery realm's best interests above all others. Now I'm getting the feeling I don't know anything at all.*

"I understand. It's the way it was with the Bittners. I did their bidding for all of those years even after I wasn't a fitting supplicant any longer."

He scoffed and shook his head. "It isn't exactly the same. They're vampires, and the Women are what keep my world in order."

"You automatically think vampires are evil, and yet you know very well Doc and Jill aren't." She continued in her mind. *I'm not saying the Women are bad, but they send you off as their lackey, and you don't seem to have much say in the matter. It was the same with the Bittners. It's true they used me as their supplicant as a child, but they were still decent to me just the way you believe the Women are to your world.*

Rooney pursed his lips but yanked her arm and sped up his walking to a rapid march.

After a few minutes, Belle dug in her heels and stopped, tugging her hand away when he tried to keep going. "I'm trying to be honest with you, Rooney. There's no reason to take your frustration out on me." She planted her hands on her knees and leaned forward to catch her breath.

His hands on her arms brought her gaze up to his. His green eyes bored into her, and she stood slowly, entranced. His lips pecked the corner of her lips. Then he slipped close to pull her into an embrace.

"I'm sorry I'm being prickly," he said close to her ear so that he only had to whisper. "It's not you, princess. I'm frickin' worried as hell about all of this. I can't imagine what we're going to find out there on that island and this weather..." His voice died off as he lifted his face to the sky, where dark clouds were whirling in little vortices and lightning flashed. "Something really wrong is happening."

"I know. I think I'm nervous, too, or I wouldn't be so sensitive to your moodiness. The rhythm of this place is changing. It's like the vibrations are out of sync."

"Hmm..." He caressed her cheek, and they started walking again, this time at a normal pace and with his arm around her shoulders. "I wish I knew more about a siren's powers. I think there's more to it than you and I know."

"Well, we can start with what I know. First off, I never knew I was a siren. I'm not even sure what that means, but anyway...I learned from about thirteen that I could get most people to bend to my will just by changing my voice. If I wanted to go shopping, I could use a special tone with Betty, and she almost never failed to give in."

"I'm not sure I like that power. It means you could manipulate me to your wiles. We've already established what a sex goddess you are, so that means you'd have me servicing..."

"Rooney!" She slapped at his arm, her face heating despite the cold air. The red-haired devil grinned, and she shook her head then took his hand to continue walking. "So as I was saying...my powers of voice don't work as effectively on vampires for some reason. There's a minute effect, but mostly they get wise to what I'm doing and it just falls apart. I can also recognize almost any magical creature. I sense a vibration from them, and each type of creature is different. That's how I knew Gerry was a succubus the first time I saw her."

She took a moment to tell him about that night, the night when Nicky and Gerry infiltrated the Bittners' party to rescue Lena, Jeremy, and Nona from the Org. Belle had helped them get past the werewolf guard Buck and then returned to the hospital along with the children. And that was how she came to meet Rooney.

"So you're like a paranormal metal detector, yet you didn't know you were a siren."

Belle shrugged, furrowing her brow. "I had no comparison for a siren. I mean, it's how a kid learns the colors. Someone points and says that's blue, and you know it's blue. No one ever pointed to someone and said that's a siren. Of course, if we're extinct, there wouldn't be anyone to point to."

Rooney cut his eyes to her, and holding his hand close to his chest, he pointed at her as if she might not notice. She couldn't help the laugh that welled up inside her. This man was forever making her laugh, and although it was a bit disconcerting at first, she found she liked the carefree feeling he elicited from her.

"Anything else? What about the humming?"

"Oh, yes, I didn't find out about that until the Bittners were fighting one day. It had Lena and Jeremy really upset. I held Jeremy close and hummed a song. Before we knew it, the sound of my voice had created a bubble and we couldn't hear anything but each other. It actually lasts about sixty seconds after I stop if I create a really strong field."

"That's pretty amazing."

"Also, there's something about this place, the faery realm. It's like I feel hypersensitive. I sense things and respond to things in a new way. For instance, that tree when we first crossed over. It was like it sent me a message via vibrations across the ground. I heard and I understood, just like that. I've never experienced it anywhere else before."

They walked along in silence for a little while, and when she glanced at him, she saw that Rooney appeared to be deep in thought and chewing his tongue. Up ahead, a long body of water was making its appearance, and Belle felt her stomach knot up when she saw whitecaps churning up due to the windy conditions.

"Have you ever thought about projecting your humming or your vibrations or whatever at someone? As a weapon?"

She blinked, forcing her mind away from the choppy sea before them. "Not really. It hadn't occurred to me. Do you think I can?" Even after the words left her mouth, she thought about the incident with the werewolf at the cabin in Danville. Had she directed her vibrating in a way that killed the were?

Rooney lifted and dropped his shoulders then pointed off to her left. "I think I see a boat dock there. Let's go find the owner and see if we can get across to the island."

Chapter
TWENTY-THREE

There was indeed a small dinghy tied next to the dock, bouncing up and down on the waves. A small cottage was just up a little hill so they made their way there to find the owner. He was a rotund elf by the name of Kato.

The man seemed a bit broody so Rooney decided to let Belle do all of the talking. She used her sweetest voice to tell him about how she and Rooney had thought it would be terribly romantic to go out on the water. He seemed unconvinced at first, especially considering the nasty weather, but before long she had him eating out of her hand.

The burning knot was growing in the pit of Roon's chest, billowing out in all directions, so his stomach churned and his throat felt choked off. He knew it was the call of the Women and that it would only get worse. They didn't have a lot of time.

"Ye be careful now. Don't be goin' too fast 'er ye'll capsize and lose me boat."

"Yes, sir," Belle assured, flashing him an innocent smile.

She was putting on a brave face, but Roon could see how nervous she was. Who wouldn't be under the circumstances? The unknown lay ahead for both of them, and it was much worse for her because the entire faery realm was new to her. He cupped the back of her head tenderly and pulled her along towards the shore.

Rooney hopped into the forward end of the boat and located the oars. The water was very choppy, lapping against the sides of the boat in rapid cadence. Belle stood on the dock and looked at him with tightly pursed lips. Her face was ashen and for a minute he thought she was going to get sick.

"You okay?"

She nodded, saying nothing, her eyes moving up and down with the movement of the boat in the water.

"C'mon, princess. It's not that bad. I've been in rougher, and I'm excellent on the water."

"You are?" Her voice was so soft he barely heard her.

"Sure. I'm a champ. We'll get over there in a cinch."

He gave her a hand to hop down into the aft of the boat. She clenched his fingers when a wave knocked them against the dock with a thud. He winked as he helped her take her seat. Ignoring the increasing pain from the pull of the Women, Rooney started rowing towards the island.

Rooney thought luck must be on their side because the wind was in their favor, helping pushing them to the shore. They were only about ten feet from land when a strong gust of wind sent the boat tilting to the side. Belle screamed and clutched at the opposite side, overcompensating.

He knew what was going to happen long before she did and there was nothing he could do to stop it. He inhaled a deep breath just before the dinghy rolled over and tossed them both into the water. Rooney was an excellent swimmer, a necessary skill for water wrestling, which was the main event in the faery world Games.

With long strokes he made his way to Belle, who was thrashing under the water, bubbles of air erupting all around her. As soon as he touched her, she clawed at him, trying to use his body to climb up to the surface. Her actions were wild and panicked, and she very nearly overwhelmed him to the point where he couldn't come up for air.

"Belle!" he gurgled, yanking at her arms to keep

her from grabbing his head and pushing him back under. "Belle, stop!"

She continued thrashing, coughing, and sputtering. After she pushed him back into the freezing water for the third time, he came up ready. He slapped her cheek, not hard enough to injure her but enough to stun her. She blinked a few times just before she started to sink under the water. Rooney grabbed her by her arms to keep her up and then pulled her close to him in a hug as his legs kicked to keep them afloat.

"Listen to me, princess. I'm an excellent swimmer. Just kick your legs and hold on to me. I'll get us to dry land. Can you trust me?"

She nodded, doing just as he said.

It took all of his energy to get them there but finally their feet were on land. He stumbled across the wet sand beyond the waves and deposited Belle there before collapsing onto his back, his arms spread wide so he could catch his breath.

A few minutes later, still panting, Rooney felt a little tickle on his arm and turned to see what it might be. A group of little pixies were standing beside him, poking him to get his attention.

It was unusual to see pixies standing on the ground. Even when not in the air, they preferred to rest on trees or flowers so as not to be trampled. Upon closer inspection, he could see that their little wings were clipped. Obviously the penalty for whatever infraction had sent them to exile on the Island Anathemusa.

"Hey there," the lead pixie said, cocking her little head at him. "We're the welcoming committee. The Women must have been particularly unhappy with you to make you swim over."

Rooney sat up onto his elbows and shook his head back and forth to get the water out of his eyes. "The Women didn't send us here. We came to see someone."

Even though they were only about two inches tall, he could see their eyes narrowing in suspicion, and a few of them backed away. Belle finally noticed them, and she practically crawled over him to get a better look at them. This seemed to frighten the little people even more.

"Listen, we're not here to cause any trouble. A friend told me I should come speak to a woman named Aoibhneas. Is there any way you could take us to her?"

"Well, it's Aoi you're here to see, eh?" a gravelly voice said from the opposite direction, and both Roon and Belle turned quickly to face a short yet wide fellow who Rooney figured was probably some sort of troll. "Leave 'em be, pixies," he advised the little people when they started tittering. "I'll take them to my cottage to warm up while you fetch Aoi."

A while later, Belle and Rooney both had a layer of blankets wrapped around their shoulders and were situated in front of a fire to get rid of the chill. The troll's name was Clarence, and he was quite hospitable even if he wasn't much for conversation. Rooney got tired of asking the fellow questions and eventually settled for silence.

You okay? he asked Belle.

She cut her eyes to him, the only part of her body visible from under the blankets. She nodded but that was all.

I'm sorry I slapped you, princess, but you seemed pretty determined to drown us both.

Again she glanced at him. Then she slid the covers down to her shoulders so she could begin raking her hands through her tangled black locks. *I know. I should've told you I couldn't swim. I don't like being helpless, Rooney.*

He grinned and winked at her. *I kind of guessed that.*

This is sort of strange, don't you think? I wonder who this Aoibhneas is exactly.

There was a knock on the cottage door and they both looked up. *Seems we're about to find out.*

Aoibhneas swept into the room like a hot breeze. Her auburn hair was pulled back at the nape of her neck, falling in long waves down her back. A few streaks of gray at her temples and the lines on her face spoke of either age or perhaps a difficult life. Still, she was glorious and exotic in her looks, her mere presence demanding attention from all occupants of the room.

Rooney stood and set his blanket aside, holding his hand out to her. "I'm Rooney, and this is Belle. McKenna said we should speak to you."

A spark of surprise flashed in her eyes, but she

shook his hand. "What exactly is developing on the mainland? Our faeries on the watchtowers have reported storms, changing weather patterns. Has something happened to the Women?"

He was surprised by her questions. He thought he was the one here to get information, not to deliver it. "I'm not sure what's going on, but I'd say the Women are alive and well at the moment."

She studied him, her green eyes slits in her examination. "They're calling you." It was a statement, not a question.

Again she caught him off guard. "Do you still have your powers?" Rooney asked in a suspicion-laced voice.

Easing her hand from his, she glanced at Belle before taking a seat at Clarence's table. The troll made himself comfortable by leaning against his front door. "I no longer have my powers. But I don't need them to see the pain behind your eyes and to recognize it for what it is. How long have you been ignoring their call?"

He glanced at Belle when she stood suddenly, worry marring her features. "You're hurt?"

Rooney waved his hand to dismiss her concerns then faced Aoi again. "I've been back here for almost twenty-four hours. They starting calling me as soon as I set foot in the faery realm."

"Set foot in the faery realm? You've crossed over then and you still possess your powers? So that means the faery-witch is real."

He took that intro to start explaining things, beginning with his task to connect with Devan so that the Women could keep her safe. Aoi listened, though her expression was cold and detached.

"And so now the Women have the faery-witch beholden to them, which makes it quite convenient to them as she holds the key to unleashing the two worlds on one another again."

It was the same thing his father had suggested. He was beginning to get the idea that everyone had a different idea about the Women than he did. There was some great secret he was being kept out of and that really pissed him off. "What the hell is going on? I wouldn't expect you to have a good opinion of the Women since you've been banished from the mainland, but what I don't understand is why everyone thinks I needed to come talk to you."

She pressed her lips into a thin line and cut her eyes to Belle.

"What about her? Is she just a pretty face or does she fit into this somehow?"

Chapter TWENTY-FOUR

Belle raised her chin and looked down at the red-haired beauty as if she were a peasant and Belle a queen. She knew she didn't like the faery from the moment she walked into the room, even if there was something enchanting about her looks.

"She's a siren, she's my woman, and she's a whole helluva lot more than just a pretty face."

It was hard not to feel smug about the way Rooney made that statement. It was no wonder she fell more and more in love with him the longer she spent with him.

Aoibhneas laughed, a shrill sound that caught all of their attention and even earned an open-mouthed gape from Clarence. "A siren. Oh, that is perfect. A siren here in the faery realm. No wonder things are spinning out of control out there. Báisteach must be beside herself."

"Are you going to explain all of this or not?" Belle spoke, her words acerbic, her eyes like big, angry black holes.

Aoi stood to face her, her own face fiery. For a moment the women stared at each other in a standoff. Then finally the redhead inclined her head with a cold smile. "Well, your highness, I suppose I shall." She motioned with her hand that Belle should sit again.

"I suppose you know that sirens are supposed to be extinct," Aoi said, taking her own seat again.

"Yeah, I know," Rooney agreed. "Belle was in the human realm. She didn't even know what she was until I told her." And he explained the way Belle could manipulate her voice and sound waves.

"A siren indeed then. Do you know how they came to be extinct?"

Belle waited to hear Rooney's answer, but he had none. He admitted he had no idea and had never even wondered about it until he met her.

"There was an uprising. In the process, every single siren was killed. Executed."

"Executed?" Belle breathed, touching her fingers to her lips.

Rooney looked as much confused as astonished. "The sirens tried to overthrow the Women? Why the hell would they do that?"

"That isn't what I said. It was the Women who rose up—or more specifically, Báisteach. You see, there was a balance in this world wherein the Women and the Siren Queen worked together in symbiosis. There were always the seasonal sectors over which Earrach, Samhradh, Fómhar, and Geimhreadh provided guidance. Báisteach was the center, the giver of water. The sirens provided the rhythm of life, the means to keep the world on a natural, even keel. All of them worked together...until Báisteach fell in love."

"Whoa, whoa..." Rooney tapped the fingers of one hand into the other. "Did you say the Siren *Queen*?"

Aoi smiled at Belle, and she felt a queer cold rush through her limbs.

"Do you want me to continue or not?" She waited for all of them to nod before speaking again. "Báisteach had a consort, a lover. Her mistake was that she *fell* in love with him, and he wasn't quite intent on faithfulness. When she discovered that he was carrying on with a siren, she became enraged. But she let her rage fester, let it grow inside her, and she took her time plotting and planning her revenge with the utmost patience. It took many years of conspiracies and ill-fated catastrophes to drum up a band of faeries against the sirens. She made this realm believe the sirens were intent on destroying us all, and before long, sirens were being murdered. They fought back, which only fueled the uprising. In the end, every last siren was done away with."

"All except Belle apparently," Rooney said, his serious green eyes boring into Belle. She shuddered, putting her arms around herself to ward off the eerie feelings overcoming her. He placed a hand upon her knee, squeezing before turning back to Aoi.

"It was believed that no sirens ever left the faery realm. They resided here on the Island Anethemusa. Apparently, at least one left before the Time of Choosing."

Belle considered this a moment in silence. Her eyes glazed over as she became lost in thought, in the memories of her childhood. After a time, she realized everyone in the room was staring at her and she felt heat creep into her cheeks.

"I don't know anything. My first memories are of an orphanage, and then I went to reside with my adoptive parents, the Bittners. I know nothing of my lineage."

Aoi's lips curled into a frigid smile. "Ah, well, it matters not who your parents were, my pretty. All sirens were considered of royal lineage, hence why they were all destroyed. Once the power grab began, Báisteach could not allow any to survive. When they were gone, her takeover was complete, and she became the central control over the faery realm. And to keep their power, the Women have employed spies to keep an eye on their perfectly contrived kingdom ever since."

"Spies?" Rooney rubbed the back of his neck, and Belle leaned forward to caress the spot for him.

"You are one of them," Aoibhneas informed him, raising an eyebrow. "I was once, until I discovered something worth more than all they could do to me. All of us here on Island Anethemusa were once answerable to the Women."

Belle felt there was some message implicit in this faery's hard gaze, and her stomach tightened when she caught the meaning. Belle was Rooney's something, the person he was risking all to be with. The one he was defying these Women to be with. She was too afraid to ask what might happen to him.

"What happened to the lover? To Báisteach's consort?" Rooney asked.

"She sent him through the golden door to the human world. She couldn't bear to kill him, I suppose, so stripping Lodar of his powers was the next best thing."

"Lodar?" Belle cried, the hand on Rooney's neck falling to her side like dead weight.

Thunder cracked nearby, and Aoi glanced up towards the ceiling then back to Rooney. "Will you go to them?"

"Do I have a choice?"

Rooney's words were laced with an ominous tone, and Belle felt a weight settle onto her shoulders.

She looked to Aoibhneas and watched in awe as the woman's shield of ice crumpled. Her green eyes glistened with tears, and her lower lip began to tremble. She clasped her hands together into a tight ball and pulled them against her chest as if holding on to some invisible talisman. "There is nowhere to hide from them. If there were a place, any place, they could not reach, I would have found it when I had the chance. There is no choice. They will find you, and the longer you delay, the worse it will be for you."

Chapter TWENTY-FIVE

Rooney knew the answer to his question before Aoi spoke. There would be no reason for her or any of the fae to be on that island if there were a way to hide from the Women. The ties that bound them to their overseers were too deep to extricate. It was time for him to pay the piper.

He focused his mind on Devan, flicked his hand in front of them, and conjured the golden door. His brunette BFF had her back to them and spun around quickly when the glow of the door bathed the room she was in with bright yellows.

"Well, I'm glad I'm fully dressed," she grumbled, planting her hand on her hip.

"Sorry, Devvie," he apologized, raking a hand through his hair. "We're in a bit of a bind here, and I need your help."

Her gold-brown eyes glistened with concern, and she stepped closer to the door, though careful not to cross the threshold. She could open a portal that would not strip a magical creature of its powers, but by all their understanding, Rooney's door between the worlds would not offer her the same protection.

He reached a hand behind him and groped for Belle. She found his fingers and squeezed them. With a deep breath, he turned his head to face the woman he loved and took his time studying her. She had that tough, stoic expression on her face, but when he touched her, something keyed up within him, and he could almost physically feel her anxiety.

"This would be so much easier if you'd let Devvie cross you back to the human realm while I do what I've got to do." His stomach lurched because even before he finished his statement, she was shaking her head.

"What's happening, Roon?" Devan demanded from the other side of the door.

He kept his eyes on Belle while he thought of how to answer that. Then he thought better about answering it at all, at least for the moment. Finally he broke contact with Belle and turned back to Aoi. "Do you think they're listening?"

"Not here. We're ignored and forgotten once we've been banished here. But they could be listening there." She motioned to Devvie.

"In the human realm?"

Aoi's smile was sad as she nodded. "Of course."

Rooney inhaled and exhaled a long forlorn sigh.

"Belle, can you do that humming thing? Can you block Devvie's voice from here?"

Belle took a few steps closer to the golden door, her eyes keen as she considered the space and distance. Finally she inclined her head with certainty. "Yes, I can." And she started humming low in her throat, the sound changing and building to different tones until she found the one she liked and motioned with her hand that he could talk.

"Okay, Devvie, here's what's happening..." He gave an abbreviated version of the things they'd discovered. His friend listened without asking too many questions, though her amber eyes flashed with fire when she realized the Women had not just been her protectors but had intended to keep her under their thumb.

"So what do you want to do?"

He appreciated that she was placing the ball in his court. She and Kent were becoming natural leaders, and now that she'd grown into her powers, it was more her inclination to call the shots. Still, in this case, they were all in virgin territory.

"I have to see the Women...like, now." He brought a hand up to his chest and rubbed absently. It was getting harder to breathe with the building fire of the Women's tug. "I'm hoping we can make a deal with them. Do we have any tags on where Lodar might be?"

Devan chewed the inside of her mouth a moment before shaking her head. "Our best guess is that he may be at the Org's underground. The other Org members have suggested that he's in charge now, but their control is crumbling as we make more rescues."

"You want to deliver him to the Women?" Belle questioned, her words almost tumbling over one another in her effort to get them out before she lost control of her bubble and started humming again.

"Yeah, that's the plan, princess. The only frickin' plan I've got at the moment. You sure you won't go back with Devvie? I'd feel better knowing you're safe. They're gonna be pretty pissed off with me."

She shook her head abruptly, her black hair falling into her face a bit. She reached to brush the locks away, but he moved faster and did it for her, kissing her ear before turning back to Devvie.

"Can we light a fire under you to try to track down Lodar? Don't go after him, just try to find out where he is."

"Anything you want, Rooney. I'll contact the team as soon as we're finished here. What else?"

He grinned and winked at her. "Just keep your clothes on, girlfriend, because if we have to make a hasty escape, I'll be poppin' in on you. 'Kay?"

Devan rolled her eyes but chuckled. Then Rooney closed the door and turned back to Belle.

"Okay, princess, you ready for this?"

She nodded and took his hand. The two of them turned back to face Aoibhneas and Clarence.

"We appreciate what you've done for us. We would never have known all of this otherwise. Is there anything we can do for you all before we leave?" he said to the auburn-haired woman.

The striking Aoi stood and put out her delicate hand. "Yes, you can. Eventually I'll call in this favor. For now, you have enough to worry about, so good luck. You'll need it."

They completed their goodbyes and stepped out of the cottage, leaving Aoi and Clarence alone. The incessant burn and pain in Rooney's chest and stomach was wearing him down, and he was afraid he would have a hard time with his magic before long. There was no longer a need to hide from the Women as they'd be practically knocking on their door anyway, so he decided to go ahead and open the golden door.

When they stepped through the portal, Belle gasped in amazement. The grey hill where the Women resided was striking to say the least. It jutted up from the perfectly flat and green ground around it like a jagged stone obelisk with stairs winding up to the top.

"They're up there?" Belle murmured, her eyes following the hill to the top.

"They're up there," he acknowledged, taking her hand and stepping over the dividing line surrounding the hill. He knew what to expect, but Belle gasped again as soon as they crossed. All outside noise became muted when one reached the vicinity of the hill. It was as if the Women were in a place wholly separate from the rest of the faery realm, and yet their influence on the world was absolute. "C'mon, princess. Up we go to face the music."

"Wait." She tugged him back, and he swallowed to tamp down the nausea of his pain so that she couldn't see it in his face. When he faced her, it was with love in his eyes and hopefully nothing else. "The children. Your parents will take care of the children if anything happens?"

"My parents would never let anything happen to those kids. I trust them unequivocally. Okay?"

She nodded but didn't let go, either with her hands or with her eyes. She locked those dark orbs onto him and clutched his soul tight. He couldn't look away even when a spasm of pain made him flinch.

"I love you, Rooney. With what I've told you about Lodar, I know I probably seem like a silly girl who latches on to anyone paying the proper attention. But I know this is real. I know I love you, even though we just met each other."

He hooked his hand around her neck and pulled her lips to meet his. It was a hard, closed-mouthed kiss that only lasted a second or two, but he knew it got his message across. "I love you too, princess."

Chapter TWENTY-SIX

Belle wasn't really sure what she'd expected to see when they reached the apex of the hill, but it certainly wasn't what was there. Four women stood in a circle in the center of the butte, each in a separate fourth of the ring. Their faces were exactly the same—quadruplets perhaps—except each of their heads was topped with differing colors of long hair: orange, brown, white, and yellow. She examined them closely and considered the things she'd learned about them from Rooney and Aoibhneas. It became clear that each woman was of a different season: Summer, Autumn, Winter, and Spring.

None of their eyes were open, all of their expressions pinched and taut. They clutched hands with each other in a grip that looked so tight as to be painful. In the middle and just above them was a black and blue ball of water that spewed clouds into the air like a volcano. Clearly the storms overcoming the entire faery realm were emanating from this liquid sphere.

"What the hell?" Rooney gritted from clenched teeth.

Belle turned to look at him, but the wind whipped around her and slapped her hair into her face. She brushed it aside, and when she finally saw the expression on his face, she realized that whatever they were seeing was not the norm.

"You have finally come," the orange-haired woman said, and Belle imagined she must be the Woman of Summer.

Rooney didn't answer, and she wondered why until he dropped to his knees, clutching his throat and wheezing to get his breath. She fell to his side, taking his face in both hands and crooning to him words of love. Her alarmed voice softened then whispered tiny endearments, singing them to him in a tone she hoped would reach him. After a moment, he opened his eyes, still pained but finally able to breathe.

"You're blocking them. They can't get to me right now because of your voice. It's you, Belle," he panted, turning his head so he could kiss her palm.

"Cease!" one of the Women cried, her words

breaking into Belle's consciousness like shards of glass.

Belle stopped her vocal ministrations and glanced over her shoulder to see the white-haired Woman staring at her with cold blue eyes.

"They told us you were a siren. It appears they were correct."

Belle felt anger rise up in the pit of her stomach, and she stood to face the Women, her hands fisted at her hips. "*They* as in your spies?" she spat, her words vitriolic.

"Do not trifle with us, girl," the Autumn Woman warned.

"We don't have enough energy to do this now," Spring spoke, pulling at her sisters' hands in both directions. "Rooney must do what we've charged him to do."

"I'll bring you Lodar," Roon agreed, crawling a few steps before working his way back to his feet. "We'll go back and get him and we'll bring him to you."

Spring's face showed her relief, and the tension in her eased a bit. When it did, the whirling orb of water at their center tried to rush free of its invisible binds, and that was when Belle realized there was a person in the center of it. A Woman, to be exact.

"Báisteach…"

It was Roon who'd whispered the name, and it finally became clear. This was the Woman at the center of it all. The Woman who had fallen in love. The

Women who had killed the sirens. The Woman whose son had been drained. The Woman who wanted Lodar handed over to her on a silver platter.

"Bring him to us alive," the Winter Woman shrilled as though reading Belle's thoughts while the four Women fought for control of Báisteach.

"Alive," Rooney agreed. "We bring him here alive and you let us go."

Autumn rolled her head side-to-side then eyed him. "Bring Lodar, and you will be free of your obligations."

She felt Roon's clammy hand take hers, and she squeezed it. "Not just free of my obligations. Free to be with Belle. You agree not wage war on this siren or any other. You will leave her alone."

The water-sphere around Báisteach roiled in agitation and the other four Women gasped and groaned and moaned as they struggled to maintain her within the sphere. Finally Winter closed her eyes and nodded her head. "So be it."

That was apparently enough for Rooney, because he turned on his heel and started dragging Belle back down the stairs. When they got to the bottom, he flicked his hand, and she knew he was conjuring the golden door.

Wind and rain pelted both of them, but when the door completely opened, they could see Devan standing on the other side, two orbs of glowing energy in each hand. Several members of the rest of her team stood behind her. They were all at the ready, prepared for whatever might be about to happen.

As jealous as she'd been of this woman just a few days ago, Belle wanted to rush her and kiss her at that moment. Never in her life had she ever had a group of friends so stalwartly defend her. And even if they weren't ready to do battle at that moment for Belle's sake, they were doing it for Rooney, and that meant the world to her.

"Are you all right?" Devan asked, her gaze darting around the area around them as if looking for foes.

"We're fine, Devvie. We just need to get across to your world and get that damned vampire so we can stay that way."

A bolt of lightened sliced the air behind them, and Belle felt the vibrations of the molecules course through her own body. A tree limb cracked and slammed to the ground. The effects of Báisteach's storm raging above them were palpable. Belle knew things would only get worse as the four Women's strength waned.

"We have to hurry," she told Rooney. "Your home can't take much more of this. She's going to destroy all of it."

Chapter
TWENTY-SEVEN

"Ack!" Rooney sputtered and gagged. "What the hell is this crap?"

Langston touched a finger to the bottom of the cup and tipped it to pour more of the awful concoction into his mouth. "All of it, my friend."

He did as he was told, but certainly not because he wanted to. Mostly because he was afraid the giant would hold him down and force feed it to him if he didn't. It was almost impossible to get his throat to swallow—the stuff was so awful—and when it hit his stomach, his muscles threatened to upchuck the contents. Still, a few swallows from the glass of water Langston handed him next and things settled down.

Releasing a huge breath, Rooney collapsed back against his chair and closed his eyes. When they'd crossed over into the hospital after seeing the Women, his entire body virtually gave out. He'd embarrassed himself by landing with a thud at Devan's feet. Then he was doubly embarrassed when Doc picked him up and carried him here to Langston's room.

He was afraid his pride would never recover.

Still, Belle was there beside him, saying not a word, caressing his head with her sweet touch. He was pretty sure if everyone would just leave them alone for, say…thirty minutes, she could make him feel all right. Of course part of him was also afraid that in his current weakened state he wouldn't be able to manage even a kiss, much less anything more.

"How do you feel?" his lovely Belle whispered in his ear.

Rooney opened one green eye and saw Langston grinning at him with a knowing smile. He ignored the shaman and rolled his head to the side to face Belle. Her face was paler than usual, evidence of her worry for him.

"Actually…" He reached a hand up and patted at his chest as if checking to make sure he was still attached to his body. "Actually, I'm better, I think."

He wasn't just putting on a brave face. Whatever the concoction was that Langston had served him, it was starting to course through his veins with super power. He flexed his fists then sat up.

"The color's returning to your complexion," Belle noted, giving his hair one last brush of her hand before standing up.

"Damn, man." He faced Langston. "That is some awesome shit. I feel like I could run a marathon."

"Pace yourself, my friend. No need to waste strength when you may need it for the fight ahead."

Rooney got to his feet and took a moment to test his legs, shifting his weight left, then right, then back again. With an abrupt nod of his head, he glanced first to the love of his life before looking back to Langston. "Is everyone ready? We need to get this show on the road."

"First things first. There are some dry clothes here for the both of you on the bed. We'll all be in the kitchen when you are ready."

When they were alone, Belle immediately started chattering and knelt at his feet to help remove his boots. "I'm pretty sure I heard Jill say they know where Lodar is. They've just been waiting for us to get here. They're all ready, every single one of them. I can't believe all of them are just instantly ready willing to do whatever it takes…"

She stopped when he reached down to stall her hands. He bent his legs into a squat so that they were eye-to-eye. Her cheeks were flushed, and the ivory of her skin stood out that much more. She was keyed up to the max, and she too was "ready to do whatever it takes." He loved her all the more for that.

"I wish we had time for me to toss you on that bed and make love to you." Her cheeks weren't just flushed now. They were flaming after he said those words. He chuckled. "I hope you don't ever lose that shy blush because it's incredibly sexy."

"It is?" she asked, her lips barely moving.

He smacked a quick kiss to those heart-shaped lips. "It is. And soon, very frickin' soon, I am going to make love to you for days on end. I guess for now we'd better both get dressed."

Before he could heave his body back to standing, she fisted her fingers into his wet shirt and pressed her mouth to his. She clutched at him, opening her mouth and insisting that he open his. The kiss turned rough, demanding, bruising. She didn't seem to mind.

It was all he could do to pull away. "Princess, you amaze me sometimes." He straightened his body, and when he looked back down at her, she quirked her gaze up to his with a coy half smile and winked. He very nearly gave in to his body's demands and tossed her on the bed after all.

A few minutes later, both of them in fresh, dry clothes, they made their way into the kitchen. The entire team was there, paired off in their respective couples and waiting patiently. Rooney let his eyes circle the room, making contact with each person. Then he focused back on Devan and lifted his eyebrows in question.

"Okay," she began. "So Langston and Kris are going to stay here with the kids while the rest of us go to the underground."

"And the big guy will be ready to get there lickity-split through the golden door if we call," Jill piped in.

Belle wrapped her arms around herself. "Do we know how many there are? What type of a crew he's gathered?"

"Nicky?" Devvie queried.

The dhampir shrugged. "We think there may be as many as two dozen. Mostly weres and lower level vamps. The bigger guys are all heading for the hills, so to speak. The rescues are happening without a fight. Seems like the smart ones know better than to fuck with the faery-witch."

"And her team," Gerry added, with strong emphasis on the word team.

"It's all of us," Kent told them. "All of you've played a part. As it is, Lodar's looking for you, Belle. He wants you back at all costs, for some reason. We're still not sure why. Having you there will ensure that he doesn't run again."

Rooney didn't like the innuendo in that statement. This wasn't supposed to be about using Belle as bait to catch the damned vampire. This was supposed to be about finding a way for them to be free.

"Don't worry, Roon," Devvie spoke, approaching and placing a hand on his shoulder. "We will all be working to protect Belle." He ground his teeth together and didn't speak. She got closer, putting her mouth just inches from his ear. He remembered a day when he would've given anything to have her this near to him. "C'mon, Roon. Pain, joy, death, life, magic. You know as well as anyone that we're in this moment because we're supposed to be. I'm the fucking faery-witch, and you're my best friend. I'm not going to let anything happen to the woman you love."

Chapter
TWENTY-EIGHT

Belle couldn't hear what Devan had said to Roon, but it must have done the trick because he nodded. They finished discussing their plans, then all got ready to go. Surprisingly, she wasn't nearly as nervous as she should have been. She'd been fighting to protect herself and her children for a long time. Having all of these people standing beside her would make this a cinch.

She hoped.

Devan opened the golden door for them, and one by one their little army stepped through. When Belle and Rooney crossed the portal, she saw that they were inside some sort of catacombs. They came through in an open area that had passageways going off in about five different directions.

"Interestingly enough," Nicky told them, "three of these all lead to the same section—the main hideout. I know it sounds pretty crazy, but Lodar has a sort of throne-room setup."

It didn't sound all that crazy to Belle. Lodar always held himself like he was better than all the rest. His overgrown sense of self-worth only increased over the last year—and especially after Belle changed her mind about marrying him.

"How do you know all this?" she asked.

"Gerry's been here with one of the weres. You remember Buck."

Belle snorted and rolled her eyes. The night she'd met Gerry and Nicky, they had to find a way to get past Buck, the werewolf the Bittners had hired to keep an eye on the children. Buck was mostly stupid and had a big crush a woman named Jo Beth. Gerry just happened to have the ability to shift into Jo Beth's body. "I'm surprised the packs would let Buck in here. None of them care for him."

"Well, he's not here now," Nicky laughed, eying his wife, who promptly smacked him. "Gerry developed a soft spot for him and convinced him to move to Alaska and get out of this business. She says he's doing very well there and has a nice plump gal who reminds him of Jo Beth."

"Okay, guys," Kent told them all, rallying their attention. "Nicky, tell us which ways to go and let's get this thing done so no one catches us before we're ready."

"This section and this one"—the dhampir pointed to two passageways—"are the ones leading around to the back so Jill and Doc can go that way and Gerry and I will go this way."

"Fine," Doc nodded, a resolute look on his face.

"Just stay to the right down each turn," Gerry told him. "No left turns."

Jill's blond curls bobbed when she inclined her head in understanding.

"This section leads directly to the throne room. Smack dab in the center of it. That's where the rest of you will go. It's still daytime, and a lot of the vamps will probably be sleeping. The weres will smell you long before you get there."

Jill, Doc, Gerry and Nicky started down their sections. Kent and Devan took places on either side of Belle, and Rooney got behind her. She turned to look at him, her eyes wide so she could take in each nuance of him.

"You okay, princess?"

"I'm okay, Rooney. Let's get this over with."

He winked and then shimmered until his body disappeared. With him invisible, they started walking. Belle's mind churned with nervousness and anticipation. She hadn't told Rooney, but she wanted to get some answers from Lodar before they captured him. Something about his unbending desire to have her nagged at the back of her mind. There must have been some reason why, and now that she knew more about herself, she wondered if that might be part of the solution.

A sliver of light appeared in the passageway, and she took a deep breath as she realized they were almost there. She wiggled her fingers in little waves, refusing to bunch them into fists because that would be too much like freezing up. And she would not freeze up this time.

About fifteen werewolves surrounded them when they broke free into the throne room, all of them shifted into their huge animal forms, fangs exposed, snarling. Belle did her best to ignore them. If Lodar wanted her that bad, then she knew he wasn't going to let his minions hurt her—at least not yet. She searched the room for him.

"Well, well." His syrupy voice echoed off the walls. The deflection of the sound confused her siren's senses. She still wasn't sure where he was, and her gaze twitched to every nook and cranny of the room in search of him. "If it isn't my darling fiancée."

"Where are you?" she cried out.

He stepped from behind a little half wall. She was reminded why he'd been able to get to her so easily. He was breathtakingly handsome, with golden blond hair that fell past his shoulders in waves and sharp Roman facial features. His body was chiseled exquisitely, and as usual, he wore clothes intended to accentuate his perfect form. He was an Adonis.

"I knew you'd come back. I just didn't expect you to bring guests. But you've made me very, very happy with your gift."

"This isn't a gift, Lodar." She shook her head, frowning. "We're here to take you back to the faery realm."

He laughed, a sound that used to turn her limbs to butter. She could remember making little jokes just so she could hear that laugh. She'd been so young and probably not nearly as funny as he'd pretended she was. His seduction of her had almost been absolute. He still made her throat go dry when he turned his ice blue eyes on her.

"Yes, and that is the gift." He waved a hand and the weres closest to Kent began to circle in closer. The man crouched low, ready to fight with the slightest provocation. "And the faery world is exactly where I intend for us to go."

Gerry and Nicky came through the back passageway about that time and the werewolves could no longer contain their desire to fight. One of them leaped a little too close to Kent, and he started shooting energy flares at them.

Devan's eyes illustrated how torn she was, but she stuck close to Belle and let Kent, Gerry, and Nicky do the fighting for now. She put a hand to her braid and ripped away the rubber band holding it together, allowing the wild strands to cascade all around her. Belle knew she derived some of her power from her magnificent hair.

She wondered where Jill and Doc were but didn't have time to focus on that question. Amidst the fighting, Lodar moved closer to them. As he approached her, her throat began to close and she felt terror rise up from her belly. She couldn't do this now. She couldn't afford to clam up and freeze.

Easy, princess. I'm here. It was Rooney's voice, and her shoulders dropped with relief.

But then she noticed Lodar's head cocked to the side and a quizzical raising of his eyebrow. He'd seen her cut her eyes to the side and behind her. Vampires move with lightning speed, and Lodar was there behind her in a flash. She screeched and grabbed his arm, trying to pull him back, but he lashed out with his claws at the place she knew Rooney was standing.

The invisibility cloak he'd had on himself dropped as soon as his skin was pierced by Lodar's vampire nails. Roon gripped his side where blood was beginning to gush. Devan jumped into action and blasted Lodar with an energy burst.

Belle rushed to Rooney's side, putting her hands atop his. "Is it bad?"

"Nah, I've had worse." He brushed her hands away and strode forward, both he and Devan facing Lodar together now.

"Do you know, my love, why you're drawn to this faery?" Lodar asked.

She stepped closer, standing between and behind Devan and Roon.

"Sirens are nymphs of the faery realm. He's one of our own." The vampire continued, clearly speaking only to Belle as his eyes were focused directly on her.

"Yes, I know you were a faery. I know what happened to you."

He stood stoically, his body not moving at all, but his eyes twitched as he gazed at her. She saw something deep in that look, something broken and hurt. Something demented and twisted, too. "And you, my beloved Belle, are the key to my return. I needed a faery strong enough to get me into the faery realm. I've sampled every faery I could find here in this world. None of them were strong enough."

"You never...you never tasted me." Her hand automatically clutched at her own neck, feeling the carotid pulsing.

Lodar laughed. "No, never. I knew the moment I saw you that you were a siren. I knew that would be enough. I would make you mine, just as Merrimarie was mine. You and I will defeat that bitch Woman."

So that was it. He wanted her because she reminded him of the siren he'd loved. He wanted her because he thought she could bring down the Women. How could he be so wrong and so blind? She was a coward and always had been. She would never be strong enough to defeat the Women.

"You're wrong. All this time you were looking for some crazy miracle, and I'm not it."

"I knew I'd find my miracle with patience. Báisteach sent me here to be powerless, so the first thing I did was find a way to become a vampire. Then I worked my way up the echelon of the Org. It wasn't easy to start at the bottom and pay those dues. And when I had the means, I started searching for and purchasing children that seemed the most promising. The boy came the closest…until you."

She swallowed, and her stomach twisted. She could see Devan and Rooney stepping closer to Lodar, and she knew they were preparing to fight. She had to keep him talking. "The boy you told me about?"

Lodar shrugged, blinking away some shred of emotion that had tried to spring up in his eyes. "Yes, Craig. He was good. Very, very good. He might have been the key if he hadn't been so small. I'd waited so long. He was a fitting lesson to me of patience. I just couldn't stop taking more and more from him. And then the little brat gave up and died on me."

The roar that reverberated off the walls caught all of them off guard, even Lodar. He glanced up just in time to see Doc pummel him to the ground. Everything seemed to start happening at once, fighting beginning in almost every direction.

Her eyes instantly focused on Rooney, who was trying to pull Doc off of Lodar. The two vampires were viciously battling, and it was clear that Doc was in it for the kill. She could hear Rooney saying something, but her mind couldn't register. She focused instead on the black-red wet area of blood soaking his shirt and down his leg. His movements were strained and he favored his wounded side. All she could think was how much she loved him and how much she wanted all of this to be over so they could be together with the children.

Peace. She wanted peace.

Belle closed her eyes and inhaled, slowly letting her head drop back and her arms go slack at her side. She searched out all of the inner vibrations from the creatures around her. She pegged each one, discerned the different species from the other. After she mentally honed in on the ones she wanted, she opened her mouth to cry out in a perfectly choreographed vibration. She absorbed every ounce of strength from her arms and her legs, directing all that she had to the very center of her.

Chapter
TWENTY-NINE

"Son of a bitch, she's doing it again!"

Rooney clapped his hands over his ears the same time Nicky did, and the two of them turned to look at Belle. Her lips were wide and she was screaming in a way he'd never heard before. She lifted her arms from her waist towards her shoulders, and as she did, her body rose a foot or so off the ground.

And she kept on screaming.

All of the weres began whining, using their paws to swipe at their ears in pain. The walls of the catacombs shook with her power, and rocks began tumbling from the ceilings. Devan, Kent, and Gerry were also holding their ears, but the effect of that scream on the vampires was astonishing. All of them, including Doc, Jill, and Lodar, turned zombie-like, their eyes glazing over and their bodies seizing where they stood.

"What's happening?" Devan cried, tugging at Rooney's shirt sleeve to get his attention.

"She's going to take the whole fucking place down is what's happening," Gerry cursed.

Nicky tried to get close to Belle, but the nearer he got, the slower he moved, as if he were trudging through molasses. "I can't get close to her. There's some sort of force field."

"She's more powerful than I realized," Rooney murmured so softly no one was able to hear him. He was in awe as he watched his beautiful Belle releasing every bit of magic she had. A kind of magic he'd never before imagined.

"The door," Devan said above the noise. "I'll open the door and we'll all get through. We've got to get Jill and Doc out before the ceiling collapses on all of us."

"And Lodar," Rooney insisted. "C'mon."

Devan opened the door and Kent started dragging Doc through while Nicky hefted Jill over his shoulders and carried her. Rooney and Gerry both took the catatonic Lodar by the feet and pulled him along too. Langston met them at the portal and took over just in time because Roon was starting to feel weak from blood loss.

"Don't let him get away, big guy. We need him."

He didn't waste time seeing if Langston agreed. He turned right back to Belle. Devan was trying to get close to her now too, but even the faery-witch couldn't seem to make a dent in Belle's field.

"I could blast her, but I don't want to hurt her," Devan told him, her face crinkled in consternation. "We've got to stop her and get her out of here, Rooney."

Rooney closed his eyes and reached with his soul towards Belle. *Princess, we've got him. We got Lodar. You can stop now.*

The screaming continued, and he snapped his eyes open to look at her. Her body dropped just a foot or so from the spot where it had been hanging in the air. He watched her mouth move, closing a little, and then she glanced down at him.

Rooney.

C'mon, Belle. You can turn it off now. We've got to get that bastard vampire back to the Women.

She nodded her head then popped her mouth closed. When she did, she cut off her scream and her body fell like a rock. Rooney orbed just beside her and caught her in his arms.

He reveled in the feel of her nuzzling her head into the crook of his neck. Even though the sounds had ended, rocks were still dropping from the ceiling, and he knew they had to get out of there. Devan touched his arm and shoved him a little towards the golden door.

He gave his BFF a quick glance and smiled.

"Rooney, I love you,'" Belle spoke, clutching him tight. The sweet magical sound of those words turned his heart to mush and made his legs feel tingly. Damned if the beautiful siren in his arms turned him so inside out that he almost tripped as he crossed through the portal again.

"Blood loss," he murmured as an excuse.

Chapter
THIRTY

Devan opened the golden door to the exact same spot below the grey hill. The faery realm looked almost wholly different though. Trees were down, limbs flung in all directions. The wind was still whipping, and the rain was coming in sheets. About a hundred yards from the hill was a river that hadn't been there before, and it churned with a black debris-filled muck that spoke of flash flooding.

Báisteach's rage was tearing the faery realm apart.

Rooney's side was bandaged, and Devan had done a quick healing job with her magic to close the wounds up. Lodar was being held in a cage of green bars that Devan controlled. She used her magic to guide the cage up the steps ahead of Belle and Roon. When they all got to the top, the four seasonal Women opened their eyes simultaneously.

"He is here," Winter said.

"We have a bargain?" Rooney asked, stepping in front of Devan and Lodar.

"You no longer trust us." Spring's eyes welled with tears, and she glanced up at her sister, still entrapped in her water-sphere.

It was Devan's turn to make demands. "They have a bargain. Say it, or I'm going to take him back to the human world with me right now."

"Yes, we have a bargain. Rooney shall be free of all obligations to the Women. Sirens will be allowed to live here in peace."

A cry tore from the center of the water-sphere before the entire orb settled and fell towards the center of the four Women.

"Will she follow your bargain?"

All eyes turned to Belle when she spoke. She held her expression apathetic, her legs wide and her hands fisted at her sides. She knew her hair was mussed, and her clothes were coated with Roon's blood, but she ignored all of that and held her stance as if she were the most powerful person on that hill. She wanted them to know she'd be ready to fight if need be.

Autumn inclined her head. "Báisteach will follow

the bargain. She will have Lodar. That will be a fitting price."

And that was when the water fell away from Báisteach's body. She lay prone a moment on the ground at the center of the other Women. She stirred, shaking the water from her hair, and then lifted her eyes to them.

Lodar huffed and grabbed at his bars, tugging them to try to break them free, but they held him without mercy.

"He's yours. I'll let him go and then you'll have to be responsible for him," Devan advised. Belle watched as she waved her hands from top to bottom and the green bars fell away. Immediately he tried to run but waves of mud erupted from the ground and captured him in a dome. They couldn't see him anymore, but he cried and screamed from within his new prison.

"You must understand why we've done what we've done." Báisteach spoke in a hoarse voice with outstretched hands, approaching Devan and tripping over her own water-logged gown. The faery-witch lowered her eyes and gave the Woman her back, heading down the stairs to leave the grey hill.

Báisteach next reached for Rooney, but he shook his head and took a step away from her. "I can't understand any of this. All that I thought I knew is wrong. I don't care what you Women do anymore, as long as you leave me and Belle the hell alone."

Belle gazed at his hand. She took it, raising her

chin to look down on the Women. The four seasons had their eyes downcast, looks of contrition on their visages. Báisteach appeared stricken but not defeated.

A feeling of dread burned in Belle's chest. Something inside told her that things were far from settled with the Women, but she and Rooney descended the hill.

When they were outside of the grey ring and back onto green grass, Devan and Rooney said their goodbyes. Belle gave them some privacy, distracting herself watching the storm clouds subside and melt into nothing until all that remained was blue sky and a lovely burning sun.

"Well, Princess, what now?"

With a warm grin, she turned back to find Rooney alone. He had his hands up behind his head in a big stretch. She figured he was just about as exhausted as she was.

"Well, I think a bath would do us both well." She looked from his bloody clothes to her own. "And I want to see the kids. I've never been away from them this long."

"We can do that."

"And then I want to find a nice warm bed to take a nap."

He nodded, locking his eyes to hers as she approached him. "We can do that, too."

"And then…" She leaned up to whisper in his ear. The naughtiness of what she wanted to do next had her blushing clear to her toes. When she looked up at him, Rooney's green eyes were dark with arousal.

"We might have to rearrange that plan a bit," he told her in a gruff voice.

Epilogue

Robbie scampered and ran along the rubble strewn around the faery realm as fast as he could. His weasel feet allowed him to leap over piles and detour around rivulets of water that still remained after the flooding subsided. He counted himself lucky that he'd been able to make his way across to the Island Anethemusa and back considering how swollen the sea was.

He reached the cabin just before sunset and found McKenna pacing the room. Her green eyes flashed when she heard the clicks of his claws on the wooden floor. She slammed the door shut and waited.

He closed his eyes and struggled to focus on the inner light McKenna had told him about. It was months ago that she'd been sitting with him, nuzzling his furry head and talking by the fire. She mentioned the light, and at first he couldn't figure out what the hell she meant. It's in you. It reminds me a lot of the way faery children look when they're first coming into their magic.

After she told him about it, he tried to figure out what it was. He studied himself, reflected on what she could possibly see. And one morning, just before McKenna returned from her evening jaunt on the night wind, it happened. He'd closed his eyes until they hurt. He saw flashes of color behind his eyelids and he clenched his eyes harder until the color turned to bright white.

His muscles started to stretch and tear and pull. It hurt. It hurt a lot, but it felt magical, and his fascination with it was something he couldn't deny. He missed magic, and if this, whatever this was, allowed him to touch it just the slightest bit, then he wanted to embrace it even with the pain.

Now, just as then, his body shifted back into human form. He became the Robbie he'd been before. Reddish brown hair, keen green eyes, and a smile that sent women's hearts fluttering. He opened his eyes and saw McKenna watching him. It was hard to detect what was behind this blonde faery's eyes, but he wanted nothing more than to believe the sight of him could cause a reaction in her.

"Did you get to her?" she asked, all business as usual.

He nodded, quickly slipping into the pair of pants she always left for him on the chair beside the door. "I got across. It wasn't easy. Damned place is a mess. I told her that they brought Lodar back to the Women. She said she's not ready yet, but soon."

McKenna bit her lip and cut her eyes to the side in thought. After a moment, she shrugged and he watched her bosom rise and fall with a deep breath. "I suppose Aoi knows what she's doing. I thought she'd be ready, but if she's not…"

He watched as his faery companion slipped out of her special coat and allowed her wings to emerge. She liked to keep them tight against her body and warm when she wasn't flying. Night was blanketing the faery world, and the wind was beginning to whistle outside the door. That was her cue to be going.

"When this is over," he said, taking a few steps closer so she could feel his breath, "it would be nice if you wouldn't have to do this every night."

She raised a golden eyebrow, and her jade eyes glimmered. "It would be nice, wouldn't it?"

He was tempted to make a move, but she slipped past him before he could talk himself into it. McKenna was nothing if not careful. With all that was happening in the faery world, she couldn't afford to put the Women on edge by shirking her duties to them. She had a sector to keep tabs on, and until Aoi gave them the go-ahead, he would just have to settle for using the fire in the hearth to keep himself warm at night.

THE
End

Acknowledgements

It is hard to believe I'm beginning my second trilogy. First and foremost I must thank the fans who fell in love with Bend-Bite-Shift; without our mutual affection for these characters, I might have let the story end with the first trilogy. Also to my husband, Danny, for your support and patience and love. To Melissa Lummis who is not only one of my best friends in the whole world, but is also my "teacher of life." To the awesome, talented, supportive, phenomenal women of Romantic Edge Books – every once in a while I look around the room and wonder how the hell I got invited to this party, but I'm so honored that all of you chose me to be a part of your writing journeys. I also have to thank my nieces and nephew who inspired some of the "kids" moments in this book. And of course, to "Roon" for making all the readers fall hopelessly in love with you.

Trivia from OLIVIA

Making Belle a siren was a shoot-from-the-hip decision. When I was writing Shifty Business she had a scene in which she screamed and I thought, "Huh, she must be a siren." So then when I got ready to write I wondered what a siren could really do. And that was when the hubby and I watched a show, probably on the history channel, about Nikola Tesla. When the episode demonstrated the use of sound waves to break a crystal glass, I decided that a siren's powers were all about vibrations.

Tesla is said to have earned a reputation as a "mad scientist" but overall his life's work is pretty fascinating. He was born 1856 and over his lifetime obtained over 300 patents. He is probably most well-known for his work on the alternating current motor, having a lasting impact on the delivery of electricity today.

Towards the end of his life Tesla was working on something called a "teleforce" weapon which the press dubbed a "peace ray" or a "death ray." He described the weapon as being able to: "send concentrated beams of particles through the free air [. . .] that they will bring down a fleet of 10,000 airplanes."

Despite the fact that Tesla became a US Citizen, when he died his property was seized by the Alien Property Custodian. I guess the US government couldn't be too careful where Tesla was concerned. Of course today Tesla's legacy continues and in 2003 Tesla Motors was founded, producing electric cars with an AC motor based on Nikola Tesla's own AC motor.

About the Author

Olivia hardin realized early on how strange she was to have complete movie-like character dreams as a child. Eventually she began putting those vivid dreams to paper and was rarely without her spiral notebooks full of those mental ramblings. Her forgotten vision of becoming an author was realized when she connected with a group of amazingly talented and fabulous writers who gave her lots of direction and encouragement. With a little extra push from family and friends, she hunkered down to get lost in the words. She's also an insatiable crafter who only completes about 1 out of 5 projects, a jogger who hates to run, and is sometimes accused of being artistic, though she's generally too much of a perfectionist to appreciate her own work. A native texas girl, olivia lives in the beautiful lone star state with her husband, danny and their puppy, bonnie.

From the Author:

I hope you've enjoyed *Sweet Magic Song*. It's wonderful to be an independent author and to publish stories that may not fit into a pre-determined mold. One challenge though, is not having traditional publicists and promotional venues. **If you've enjoyed this book, please consider leaving a review or comment where ever you purchased this book or on Goodreads. And please visit www.olivia-hardin.com for more updates.**

~Olivia